CORNISH
FOLK TALES

MERRYN PETROCK

Front Cover Illustration by Nicole Omernick

Copyright © 2016 Dream Fulfilment Ltd

Introduction

Cornish Folktales have been handed down over many generations, firstly by word of mouth and later by being recorded in written form. This book presents a fairly comprehensive selection of the best, culled from recordings made in the late 19th century.

I have tried to maintain the sense of time in these stories but I have also attempted to make them more easily read by today's readers. To that end I have had to remove some of the unsuccessful efforts that were used to portray 'old Cornish' both in vocabulary and accent. To have left them in their original state would have meant providing a dictionary and, regrettably, no such document exists for the time.

You should be aware that many of these tales are quite 'dark' in content - they are certainly not always sweetness and light.

Folk Tales is one of a series of collections of Cornish Tales. Others include Fairy Tales and Legends. Taken together they provide a pretty all-inclusive collection of genuinely representative Cornish stories from the past. I hope you enjoy them.

Merryn Petrock
Launceston 2016

TABLE OF CONTENTS

THE TALE OF JOHN PENDENNIS

THERE was once a man and a woman living in the parish of St. Buryan, in a place called Tregagwith. Work became scarce, so the man said to his wife, 'I will go search for work and you live here on the savings we have.' So he took leave of her and travelled toward the East. At last he came to the house of a farmer and asked for work.

'What work can you do?' asked the farmer.

'I can turn my hand to almost anything,' said John. The farmer offered him three pounds for the year's wages and John accepted.

When the end of the year came the farmer showed him the three pounds. 'John,' he said, 'here's your wage but if you will give it back to me I'll give you a piece of advice instead.'

'Give me my wage,' said John.

'No, I won't,' said the farmer. 'I'll give you my advice.'

'Tell it to me, then,' said John.

Then said the farmer, 'Never leave the old road for the sake of a new one.'

After that they agreed for another year at the old wages and at the end of it John took instead a piece of advice and this was it: 'Never lodge where an old man is married to a young woman.'

The same thing happened at the end of the third year, when the piece of advice was: 'Honesty is the best policy.'

But John would not stay longer because he wanted to go back to his wife.

'Don't go to-day,' said the farmer. 'My wife will be baking tomorrow and she'll make you a cake to take home to your good woman.'

And when John was going to leave, the farmer said, 'Here is a cake for you to take home to your wife and, when you are most happy together, then break the cake and not before.'

So John said goodbye to him and set off homeward. At last he came to Bridestowe and there he met three merchants from his own parish, coming home from Exeter Fair. 'Hello John!' they said. 'Come with us. We are glad to see you. Where have you been so long?'

'I have been in service,' said John, 'and now I'm going home to my wife.'

'Oh, come with us! You'll be very welcome.' But when they took the new road John remembered the farmer's advice and kept to the old one. And robbers fell upon them before they had gone far from John as they were going by the fields of the houses in the meadow. They began to cry out, 'Thieves!' and John shouted out 'Thieves!' too. And when the robbers heard John's shout they ran away and the merchants went by the new road and John by the old one till they met again at Launceston

'Oh, John,' said the merchants, 'we are grateful to you but for you we would have been robbed. Come and lodge with us, at our expense, as our way of saying thank you.'

When they came to the place where they were to stay, John said, 'I must see the host.'

'The host,' they cried; 'what do you want with the host? Here is the hostess and she's young and pretty. If you want to see the host you'll find him in the kitchen.'

So he went into the kitchen to see the host. He found him; a weak old man turning the spit. Once again he recalled the farmer's advice.

'Oh! oh!' said John, 'I'll not stay here, but will go next door.'

'Not yet,' said the merchants, 'have dinner with us at least.'

Now it happened that the hostess had plotted with a certain monk in Launceston to murder the old man in his bed that night while the rest were asleep and the two of them agreed to blame it on the merchants. While John was in bed next door, there was a hole in the gable of the house and he saw a light through it. So he got up and looked and heard the monk speaking.

'I had better cover this hole,' said the monk, 'or people in the next house may see our deeds.' So he stood with his back against it while the hostess killed the old man.

But meanwhile John took out his knife and, putting it through the hole, cut a round piece off the monk's robe. The very next morning the hostess raised the cry that her husband was murdered and as there was nobody in the house but the merchants, she declared they ought to be hanged for it.

So they were arrested and carried off to prison where, at last, John found them. 'John,' they cried, 'you would not believe our bad luck. Our host was killed last night and we are going to be hanged for it.'

John said to the guards, 'Tell the justices to detain the real murderers.'

'Who knows,' they replied, 'who committed the crime?'

'Who committed the crime?' said John. 'If I cannot prove who committed the crime, hang me in their place!'

He told them what he had heard and seen and brought out the piece of cloth from the monk's robe. With that the merchants were set at liberty and the hostess and the monk were seized and hanged.

Then they came all together out of Launceston and the merchants said to him: 'Come with us as far as Penzance.' At Penzance their two roads separated and though the merchants wished John to go with them, he would not go with them, but went straight home to his wife.

And when his wife saw him she said, 'You are home in the nick of time. Here's a purse of gold that I've found. It has no name but I'm sure it belongs to the lord. I was just thinking what to do when you came.'

Then John thought of the third piece of advice and he said 'Let us go and give it to the lord.'

So they went up to his house, but the lord was not in, so they left the purse with the servant that minded the gate. Then they went home again and lived quietly for a time.

But one day the lord stopped at their house for a drink of water and John's wife said to him: 'I hope your lordship found your lordship's purse quite safe with all the money in it.'

'What purse is that you are talking about?' said the lord.

'It's your lordship's purse that I left at your house,' said John.

'Come with me and we will investigate this,' said the lord.

So John and his wife went up to the house and there they pointed out the man to whom they had given the purse. He had kept it for himself but luckily had not spent any of the money. The lord made him give it up and sent him away from the castle. And the lord was so pleased with John that he made him his servant in the place of the thief.

'Honesty's the best policy!' said John to his wife, as they danced about in their new home. 'How happy I am!'

Then he thought of the farmer's cake that he was to eat when he was most happy and when he broke it, to his great surprise, inside it was his wages for the three years he had been there.

REEFY, REEFY RUM

A SMALL girl called Nancy Parnell came down from Wadebridge to Padstow one St. Martin's summer to stay with her Grannie.

The Grannie was old and weak in her legs and could not take her granddaughter out to see the sights of the little old-world town, with its narrow streets and ancient houses, so the child had to go by herself.

When she had seen all there was to be seen in the town, she went up to look at the church, of which she had heard from her mother, who was a Padstow woman and the quaint little figures on the buttresses of the south wall.

It was between the lights when she got there, but she could see the carved figures quite distinctly, which were a lion with its mouth wide open, a unicorn with a crown encircling its neck and a young knight, standing between them, holding a shield; and when she had taken them all in she repeated a funny old rhyme which her mother told her she used to say when she was a little maid and lived at Padstow. The rhyme was as follows :

'Reefy, reefy rum,
Without teeth or tongue;
If you'll have me,
Now I am a-come.'

The rhyme - a taunt and an invitation in one - was very rude and so was the little girl who repeated it but the lion, the unicorn and the little knight did not take any notice of her and looked straight before them as they had done ever since they were carved on the wall. But Nancy was somewhat afraid of the effect of the rhyme on those quaint little figures, especially on the open-mouthed lion, who had no sign of teeth or tongue. She ran round the great square-turreted tower and took refuge under the roof of the gateway and sat on the bench to see if they would leave their stations on the wall and come after her but they did not.

The little stone knight and the two animals had a strange fascination for the little Wadebridger and the next evening again found her in the beautiful churchyard gazing up at them with her bright child-eyes and as she gazed she repeated the same rude rhyme :

'Reefy, reefy rum,
Without teeth or tongue;
If you'll have me,
Now I am a-come.'

But they took not the smallest notice of her, nor of her rhyme and the young knight did not lift as much as an eyelash but the child, now the rhyme was said, was even more apprehensive than ever of the effect it might have and ran round the tower and again took refuge in the old gateway and waited to see if they would come down from the wall and try to catch her; but they never came.

The last evening of her stay at Padstow, Nancy went once more to the churchyard to have another look at the figures and to taunt them with having no teeth or tongue. It was not quite so late as the first two evenings she had come thither and the robins were singing their evensong in the churchyard trees.

As she stood staring up at the figures, a shaft of light from the sun setting between the trees fell across their faces and the eyes of the little knight seemed to look down in sad reproach at the rude little maid as she again repeated the rhyme which was even ruder than she knew.

Her voice was shrill and loud and was heard above the robins' cheerful song. She had hardly finished the rhyme when she saw the lion move from his place on the wall, followed by the unicorn and the young knight and come sliding down. She did not wait to see them reach the bottom, for she took to her heels and ran for her life, but she could hear the figures carved in stone coming after her as she flew round the tower and her heart was beating faster than the church clock when she reached the gateway.

The gate, fortunately for her, was open wide and she caught hold of it and banged it behind her as the lion with his gaping mouth came up to it. She looked over her shoulder as she turned to run down the street and she saw the three figures all in a row. The young knight in the middle held his shield, gazing at her through the round wooden bars of the gate. The lion looked savage and but for the brave little knight with his pure young face, who seemed to have a restraining power upon both animals, he might have broken the bars and come through the gate and eaten the child who had invited them three times to come down and have her!

The little Wadebridger ran back to her Grannie and told her about the rhyme she had said to the little stone figures on the wall of Padstow Church and how they had come down and run after her to the gate. Her good old Grannie said it would have served her right if they had broken the gate and got her. 'A lesson to you, my dear,' she cried, 'never to be rude to man or beast, especially to figures carved on church walls.'

The three little stone figures stood all in a row on the gate step till the child was out of sight and finding she did not return, they went back to their places on the buttresses of the grey old church and there they are still. As far as we know, they have never left them since Nancy Parnell, the little Wadebridger, repeated 'Reefy, reefy rum' three times and that was when our great-great-grandmothers were children.

THE LITTLE HORSEMEN OF PADSTOW

AT the bottom of the same old town there is a house which has two tiny little men on horseback on the top of its roof. They have stood there for hundreds of years and they never leave their places except when they hear the great church clock strike the hour of midnight, when, it is said, they leave the red tiles and gallop round the market-place and through the streets of the little town.

These gallant little horsemen have seen the house on which they stand almost rebuilt; changed from an old-world building with quaint windows and doors into quite a modern one and they have the sorrow of knowing that the only things left that are ancient are the walls, the red tile-ridge, their little horses and themselves.

Long generations of Padstow children have seen these quaint little men on horseback and many a question have they asked concerning them; but the only thing they ever learnt was that whenever they hear the church clock strike twelve in the middle of the night they come down from the roof, gallop round the market and through the streets. But as children are generally in bed at that late hour, none were ever fortunate enough to see them do this wonderful feat, except little Robin Curgenven, the son of a toymaker and it happened like this:

One evening when Robin was about nine years old his father and mother went to a party; and as it was a party only for grown-up people, they left him at home asleep in bed.

Robin slept sound as a ringer till just before twelve, when he awoke and, finding he was alone in the house, he crept out of bed, opened the front door, which was just under the roof and went out and stood on the top of an external stone stairway which led down to the market-place.

The house where he lived was as quaint and old as the one on which the little men rode so gallantly and it faced it. As he stood at the head of the steps the church clock began to strike the hour of midnight. It had only struck four or five when he remembered what he had heard about those wonderful little horsemen and their steeds and he looked across the market to see if what he had been told about them was really true.

He could see the house quite plainly and the little horses and horsemen, for it was a clear night and full moon. The moment the clock had done striking Robin saw, to his great delight, the two little men on their two little horses leave the housetop and leap into the street and go galloping round and round the market-place as his parents assured him they did when they heard the clock strike twelve.

The little horses galloped so funnily and the tiny riders sat so bolt upright on their quaint little steeds, that Robin laughed to see them and said they looked exactly like the wooden toy horses and horsemen in his father's shop. And as they went galloping, galloping that queer little gallop, he clapped his hands and cheered like a Cornishman.

The tiny little horsemen took no notice of the excited boy on the top of the stairs and the moment they had finished their gallop round the old market they came through the narrow opening at the foot of the stairs and galloped away up the street as fast as they could.

So excited was little Robin Curgenven when he saw the tiny horsemen gallop away that he flew down the steps and tore after them, quite forgetting that his feet were bare and that he had nothing on except his little white nightshirt.

He ran very fast but, as fast as he ran, he could not overtake those swift little horses and by the time he got to the bottom of Middle Street they were nearly at the top.

When they reached the head of that street the tiny horsemen pulled up their horses for a minute outside an ancient-looking house with a porch-room set on wooden pillars and then they turned up Workhouse Hill and disappeared.

Robin ran faster than before and the tails of his little nightshirt flew out behind him on the wind as he ran and he never stopped running till he was half-way up Church Street, when he saw the little horses and their riders galloping down towards him.

They had been to the head of the town and were returning; and he got on the footpath and stood near an arched passage and waited for them to pass.

He did not have to wait long and so fast did they come you would have thought they were having a race. They seemed to be enjoying their gallop through the streets of the sleeping old town and Robin, as he fixed his bright young eyes upon them, saw, or thought he saw, a broad grin on their queer little faces as they galloped by.

The barefooted little lad, in his little night-garment, ran beside the quaint little horses and the little horsemen for a short distance, but they galloped much faster than he could run and soon outdistanced him and, run as hard as ever he could, he could not overtake them, but he heard the ringing of the tiny horses' hooves on the hard road as they went galloping down through the town.

When he reached the bottom of the town and the house where the little men and their horses usually stood, he glanced up and to his surprise saw them standing on the tile-ridge, looking as if they had never left it.

Robin gazed at them till he began to feel cold and then he went back across the market to his own house; and half an hour later, when his father and mother came home from the party, they found him fast asleep on one of the steps with his toes tucked up under him.

'The funny little horses and little horsemen did hear the clock strike twelve and galloped round the market and through the town same as you told me,' said Robin in a sleepy voice, when his father picked him up and carried him into the house. 'I saw them with my own eyes and I ran after them up as far as Church Street. They galloped so funnily and so fast. I am glad I saw them.'

'So am I,' said his father, laughing, thinking his small son had dreamt it as he lay asleep on the step. 'You are the first little chap who ever saw them come down from the roof and gallop and I fancy you will be the last.'

Little Robin Curgenven may have been the first to see them gallop as his father said, but he may not be the last, for the quaint little horses and horsemen are still on the roof of the house and it is told that they still gallop through Padstow streets and round what once was the market, when they hear the church clock strike twelve!

THE OLD SKY WOMAN

WHEN winter brought the cold north wind and the snowflakes began to fall, the little Cornish children were always told that the Old Woman was up in the sky plucking her Goose.

The children were very interested in the Old Sky Woman and her great White Goose and they said, as they lifted their soft little faces to the grey of the cloud and watched the feathers of the big Sky Goose come whirling down, that she was a wonderful woman and her Goose a very big Goose.

'I want to climb up to the sky to see the Old Woman plucking her Goose,' cried a tiny boy; and he asked his mother to show him the great Sky Stairs. But his mother could not, for she did not know where the Sky Stairs were, so the poor little boy could not go up to see the Old Sky Woman plucking the beautiful feathers out of her big White Goose.

'Where does the Old Woman keep her great White Goose?' asked another child, with eyes and hair as dark as a raven's wing, as he watched the snow-white feathers come dancing down.

'In the beautiful Sky Meadows behind the clouds,' his mother said.

'What is the Old Sky Woman going to do with her great big Goose when she has picked her bare?' queried a little maid with sweet, anxious eyes.

'Stuff it with onions and sage,' her Grandfather said.

'What will she do then with her great big Goose?' the little maid asked.

'Hang it up on the great Sky Goose-jack and roast for her Christmas dinner,' her Grandfather said.

'Poor old Goose!' cried the little maid.

'I don't believe the Old Sky Woman would be so unkind as to kill and pluck her great big Goose,' said a wise little maid with sunny hair and eyes as blue as the summer sea. 'Winter-time is the Sky Goose's moulting time and the Old Sky Woman is sweeping out the Sky Goose's house with her great Sky Broom and the White Goose's feathers are flying down to keep the dear little flowers nice and warm till the north wind has gone away from the Cornish Land.'

'Perhaps that is so, dear little maid,' her Grandfather said.

THE IMPOUNDED CROWS

A SMALL boy called Jim Nancarrow was sitting one day eating a pasty on top of the Crow Pound, a large enclosure built on a common by the far-famed St. Neot to impound the pilfering crows of the parish that bears his name.

Jim was the son of a thatcher and he was waiting to accompany his father to a distant hamlet to help him to thatch a cottage. He looked a nice little lad in his clean white smock, yellowish-brown breeches and a soft felt hat that was much the worse for wear shading his bright young face and clear blue eyes.

As he was waiting for his father and eating his pasty, which his mother had given him for his dinner, he saw a crow flying over Goonzion Downs, of which the Crow Pound common was a part.

As he watched it he thought of the pilfering crows which, according to the old tale, little St. Neot impounded there from morning till evening on Sundays, that his people might go to church undisturbed by fear of the great black thievish birds which ate up the corn sown in their fields. Jim had often heard this story from the old people of the parish and whenever he saw a crow he wondered if it were a relation of the wicked crows their patron Saint had impounded.

The crow that the boy was watching was flying in the direction of the Crow Pound and when it came near it alighted on the top of the wall quite close to the lad.

The crow was lean to look at with very sparse feathers and such a sorry-looking bird that Jim broke off a piece of his pasty and threw to him, which he ate as if he were starving.

'One would think you were one of the pilfering crows of St. Neot's time,' said Jim, tossing him another piece of his pasty.

To his surprise, the bird answered back, 'I am!'

17

'Are you?' cried Jim, staring hard at the crow. 'Well, you look ancient enough to be one of those birds, though I have always understood that our patron Saint lived ever so long ago, when Alfred the Great was a little chap like me. But perhaps crows tell lies as well as pilfer.'

'If I am not one of the identical crows St. Neot was unkind enough to put into this pound,' croaked the big black bird, eyeing Jim and his pasty with his bright little eye, 'I am a descendant of theirs in the direct line. I truly am,' he said, as the lad stared as if he did not believe the assertion. 'Those poor impounded crows learnt the language of men during the long hours of their imprisonment, listening to all the little Saint and his people said about them outside this pound and they passed on their dearly-bought knowledge to their children through long generations.'

'Then you are quite "high learnt," as the old men say,' cried Jim, gazing up at the bird in open-eyed amazement.

'I confess I am,' returned the crow with due modesty, 'especially in the old Cornish tongue, in which I can swear roundly. I am not going to use bad language now,' as Jim took up a stone to throw at him. 'You would not understand it if I did. I am also "high learnt" in the needs of the body and I shall be ever so grateful for a bit more of your pasty. It isn't nice to have an aching void inside one's little feather jacket.'

'I suppose it can't be,' said the lad, dropping the stone and breaking off a large piece of his pasty to toss to the bird.

He was a good-hearted little fellow and the crow's quaint appeal touched him and the sorry-looking bird, with his bedraggled tail, had most of his pasty.

'I have had a good meal for once in my life and am full fed,' said the crow, when the last of the pasty was eaten; and he perched on a stone, starred with stonecrop and fluffed out all the feathers he possessed and looked with a comical expression at Jim.

'I am better fed than little St. Neot after his poor little meal of fish,' he continued, still eyeing the boy, 'and I am feeling so comfortable that I am inclined for a chat.'

'Are you?' cried Jim, who thought this great black crow was a wonderful crow, which he certainly was. 'I don't know what to yarn about.'

'I do, then,' answered the bird quickly. 'I suppose you have heard the old tale how the little St. Neot put the poor crows into this pound.'

'Yes, I have heard about it from the old men and old women here at Churchtown,' said Jim, turning his face towards a little village close to the church, which he could just see from where he was sitting. 'But they never made much of a story of it.'

'Didn't they? Then perhaps you would like to hear the crows' version of the old tale,' said the crow. 'It will tell you that their morals were not so black as the farmers in this parish made out to the Holy Man.'

'I don't mind, if you are quick about it,' said Jim. 'I am going to a farm with my father to help him do some thatching when he has finished his dinner.'

'I cannot be driven after such a heavy meal of pasty,' croaked the crow; 'and if I may not take my time, I won't tell it at all.'

'As you like,' cried Jim with fine indifference; but the bird was anxious to tell the tale and he began :

'We crows always considered it within our right to take what we could,' said the crow, 'and pilfering, as the farmers hereabouts were pleased to call it, was the only way the crows had of picking up a living and they watched their opportunity to take what they needed to satisfy their hunger when the farmers were not about. But back in those faraway days when St. Neot dwelt here to try and make people good, times were dreadfully bad, especially for crows. The people were all tillers of the land in those days and lived by the sweat of their brow, as crows did by pilfering. There was no other way open to them and the farmers had their eyes on the land and on us poor hungry birds from dawn to dark, except on the Rest Day; and the only chance the crows had of filling their stomachs was on Sunday, when the people went to church.

The starving crows looked forward to Sunday as only poor starving birds with empty crops could and the moment one of the elder crows gave the signal, which he did in the crow way, they all flew off to the corn-sown fields and had a regular feast. My word! And didn't they feed! They picked out with their sharp beaks every grain of corn they could find.

When the farmers found out the hungry crows had eaten up all the corn they had sown, there was the Devil to pay and the poor crows were cursed from one end of the parish to the other.

The farmers resowed their fields, but they took good care to watch and see that the crows did not rob them of their toil. They were always about on the corn-sown land, Sundays as well as week-days. The crows had to go supperless to bed and little St. Neot had to preach to bare walls.

The Saint was greatly distressed at his people's neglect of their religious duties and he told them how wicked it was to stay away from church. The people said they were sorry, but declared it was the fault of the pilfering crows.

"The pilfering crows!" cried the Holy Man. "What have the crows to do with your stopping away from the House of God?"

"Everything," answered the farmers and they told little St. Neot that whenever they sowed bread-corn in their fields the wicked crows came and ate it all up and that if he could not prevent them from doing this wickedness, they must keep away from church and watch their fields. "We and our children must have bread to eat," they added, which was true enough true for crows as well as men.

'The Holy Man was very upset to hear the cause of their not coming to church and he said he would devise some means to prevent the crows from robbing the fields whilst they were attending to their worship.

St. Neot was as good as his word and the gossip in the parish was that he was building a great square enclosure of moorstone and mould about half a mile from the church. When it was finished, he told his wondering people it was a pound for crows, which he meant to impound on Sundays from dawn till dusk, so that the farmers might come to church and worship without having their minds disturbed by fear of those black little robbers eating their corn.

There was a fearful to-do among the poor hungry crows when they learned what St. Neot had done and although they knew they were within their right to steal when they were hungry and they were always hungry, poor things, they were sorry they ate up the corn the farmers had sown and every crow looked forward to the coming Rest Day with fear and trembling.'

'Well, Sunday came, as Sundays will,' continued the crow, 'and before the sun had risen little St. Neot made known his will to the crows that they were to come to be impounded and such power had the Saint over beast and bird that the crows had no choice but to obey. Long before St. Neot's bell rang out to call his people to worship in the little church, which he had built for them by the aid of his two-deer team and one-hare team, all the crows in the parish came as they were bidden to be impounded in the Crow Pound.

'And, my gracious! what a lot of them came! There were crows of all sorts and conditions, all ages and sizes! There were great-great-great Granfer and Grannie Crows! There were great-great Granfer and Grannie Crows! Great Granfer and Grannie Crows by the score! Grannie Crows by the hundred! Mammie and Daddy Crows by the thousand! And as for the children and great-great-grand-children, they could hardly be counted! Even poor little Baby Crows, just able to fly, were there!

The Crow Pound was chock-full of crows and all the place was as black as St. Neot's gown. And as for the noise they made, it was enough to turn the Holy Man's brain; but it didn't.

The little Saint did not expect to see so many crows, it was certain, though he expected a goodly number, by the big enclosure he had made; and the old tale says that, when he saw so many birds, he exclaimed with uplifted hands, "My goodness! What a lot of crows!" and he looked round at this great assemblage all in respectable black in open-eyed amazement.

The people who came flocking to church when they heard that the crows were safe in the Crow Pound were almost as astonished as St. Neot to see such a big congregation of birds.

The church was too far away from the pound for the crows to hear the little Saint preaching, but when the wind blew up from Churchtown they could hear the singing and to show you they were not so bad as the farmers made out to the Holy Man, they croaked as loud as ever they could when Mass was sung and were as silent as the grave during the time St. Neot was preaching.

Every year, from sowing time till the corn was reaped and safe in the barn, the crows were impounded every Sunday from the early morning till evening whilst little St. Neot lived.'

'Is that all?' asked Jim, who listened to the crow's version of the old tale till it was finished.

'Yes,' answered the great black bird with a croak and when he had said that he took to his wings and flew away as fast as he could fly over Goonzion Downs, the way he had come.

'That sad-looking crow did not tell the old tale half bad,' said Jim to himself, as he watched the bird fly away. 'Shouldn't I like to have seen this old pound full of crows! It must have been terribly funny when St. Neot looked in upon them and cried, "My goodness! what a lot of crows!" It must have been as good as a Christmas play. There, father is coming. That sharp-eyed old crow must have seen him climbing the hill.'

LEGEND OF THE PADSTOW DOOMBAR

IN a far-away time Tristram Bird of Padstow bought a gun at a little shop in the quaint old market, which in those days opened to the quay, the winding river and the St. Minver sandhills. When he had bought his gun he immediately began to shoot birds and other poor little creatures.

After a while he grew more ambitious and told the fair young maids of Padstow that he wanted to shoot a seal or something more worthy of his gun. So one bright morning he made his way down to Hawker's Cove, near the mouth of the harbour.

When Tristram got there he looked about him to see what he could shoot and the first thing he saw was a young maid sitting all alone on a rock, combing her hair with a sea-green comb.

He was so overcome at such an unexpected sight that he quite forgot what had brought him to the cove and could do nothing but stare.

The rock on which the maiden sat was covered with seaweed and surrounded by a big pool which was known as the Mermaid's Glass.

She was apparently unaware that a good-looking young man was gazing at her with his bold dark eyes. As she combed her long and beautiful hair she leaned over the pool and looked at herself in the Mermaid's Glass and the face reflected in it was startling in its beauty and charm.

Tristram Bird was very tall - six feet three in his bare feet - and being such a tall young man he could see over the maiden's head into the pool. Her face, in its setting of golden hair reflected in the clear depths, entirely bewitched him and so did her graceful form, which was partly veiled in a golden raiment of her own beautiful hair.

As he stood gazing at the bewitching face looking up from the Mermaid's Glass, its owner suddenly glanced over her shoulder and saw Tristram staring at her.

'Good-morning to you, fair maid,' he said, still keeping his bold dark eyes fixed upon her, telling himself as he gazed that her face was even more bewitching than was its reflection.

'Good-morning, sir,' she replied.

'Combing your hair out in the open?' he said.

'Yes,' she said, wondering who the handsome youth could be and how he came to be there.

'Your hair is worth combing,' he said.

'Is it?' she said.

'It is, my dear,' he said. 'It is the colour of oats waiting for the sickle.'

'Is it?' she asked.

'Yes; and no prettier face ever looked into the Mermaid's Glass.'

'How do you know?' she asked.

'My heart told me so,' he said, coming a step or two nearer the pool, 'and so did my eyes when I saw its reflection looking up from the water. It bewitched me.'

'Did it?' she laughed, tilting her chin.

'Yes,' he said, with an answering laugh, drawing another step nearer the pool.

'It does not take a man of your breed long to fall in love,' said the beautiful maid, with a toss of her golden head and a curl of her sweet red lips.

'Who told you that?' asked the love-sick young man, going as red as a poppy.

'Faces carry tales as well as little birds,' she said.

'If my face is a tale-bearer, it will tell you that I love you more than heart can say and tongue can say,' he said, drawing even nearer to the pool.

'Will it?' she said, combing her golden hair with her sea-green comb.

'Indeed it will and must,' he said; 'for I love you with all my soul and I want you to give me a lock of your golden hair to wear over my heart.'

'I do not give locks of my hair to landlubbers!' she cried, with another toss of her proud young head and a scornful curl of her bright red lips.

'A landlubber!' he said, with an angry flash in his bold black eyes. 'Who are you to speak so scornfully of a man of the land? One would think you were a maid of the sea.'

'I am,' she said, twining the tress of her hair she had combed round her shell-pink arm.

'No sea-maid is half as beautiful as you,' said Tristram Bird, incredulous of what the maid said. 'But, maid of the sea or maid of the land, I love you, sweet and I want you to be my wife.'

'Want must be your master, sir,' she said, with an angry flash in her sea-blue eyes.

'Love is my master, sweet maid,' he said. 'You are my love and you have mastered me.'

'Have I?' she asked, with a little toss of her golden head.

'Yes,' he said, 'and now I have told you that you are my love, and I want you to marry me, you will give me a lock of your golden hair, my sweet?'

'I cannot,' she said.

'Give me one little golden wire of your hair, if you won't give me a lock,' he pleaded, coming close to the edge of the pool. 'I will make a golden ring of it,' he said, 'and wear it for everyone to see'

'Will you?' she said.

'I will, my dear,' he said.

'But I will not give you a hair of my head even to make a ring with,' she said.

'Then give me one for a leading-string,' he said. 'If you will, my charmer, you shall take the end of it and lead me wherever you like.'

'Even to the whipping-post?' she said.

'Even to the whipping-post,' he said. 'So you will be my fair bride, won't you, my sweet? If you will consent to love me, I'll make you as happy as the day is long.'

'Will you?' she cried, with a warning look in her sea-blue eyes and a strange little laugh.

'Yes,' he said, thinking her answer meant consent. 'And I've got a dear little house at Higher St. Saviour's, overlooking the river and Padstow Town low in the valley.'

'Have you?' she said.

'I have,' he said. 'And the little house is full of handsome things: a chestful of linen which my own mother wove for me on her loom against the time I should be wed to a pretty maid like you, an oaken dresser with every shelf full of china and a cosy settle where we can sit hand in hand talking of our love. You will marry me soon, won't you, my sweet? The little house and all that's in it, is waiting for my charmer.'

'Is it?' cried the beautiful maid, taking up another tress of her golden hair and slowly combing its silken length with her sea-green comb. 'But let me tell you once and for ever, I would not marry you if you were decked in diamonds and your house a golden house and everything in it made of jewels and set in gold.'

'Wouldn't you?' cried Tristram Bird, in great amazement.

'I wouldn't,' she said.

'You are a strange young maid to refuse an upstanding young man like me,' he said, 'who has a house of his own, to say nothing of what is inside it. Why, dozens of fair young maidens in Padstow would have me tomorrow if I was only to ask them.'

'Then ask them,' cried the beautiful maid, turning her proud young head and looking out towards Pentire, gorgeous in its spring colouring.

'But I can't ask any of them to marry me when I love you,' cried the infatuated youth. 'You have bewitched me and no other man shall have you. If I can't have you living, I'll have you dead. I came down to Hawker's Cove to shoot something to startle the natives of Padstow Town and they will be startled, sure enough, if I shoot a beautiful little vixen like you and take you home to them.'

'Shoot me if you will, but marry you I will not,' said the beautiful maiden, with a scornful laugh. 'But I give you fair warning that if you shoot me, as you say you will, you will rue the day you did your wicked deed. I will curse you and this beautiful haven, which has been a refuge for ships from the time that ships sailed upon the seas;' and her sea-blue eyes looked up and down the estuary from the headlands that guarded its mouth to the farthest point of the blue, winding river.

'I will shoot you in spite of the curse if you won't consent to be mine,' cried the bewitched young man.

'I will never consent,' said she.

'Then I will shoot you now,' he said and Tristram Bird lifted his gun and fired and the bullet entered the poor young maiden's soft pink side.

She put her hand to her side to cover the gaping wound the shot had made and as she did so she pulled herself out of the water and where the feet should have been was the glittering tail of a fish!

'I have shot a poor young Mermaid,' Tristram cried, 'and woe is me!' and he shivered like one when somebody is passing over his grave.

'Yes, you have shot a poor Mermaid,' said the maid of the sea, 'and I am dying and with my dying breath I curse this safe harbour, which was large enough to hold all the fighting ships of the Spanish Armada and your own. It shall be cursed with a bar of sand which shall be a bar of doom to many a stately ship and many a noble life and it shall stretch from the Mermaid's Glass to Trebetherick Bay on the opposite shore and prevent this haven of deep water from ever again becoming a floating harbour except at full tide. My ghost will haunt the bar of doom that my dying curse shall bring until your wicked deed has been fully avenged!'

And looking round the great bay of shining waters, laughing and rippling in the eye of the sun, she raised her arms and cursed the harbour of Padstow with a bitter curse and Tristram shuddered as he listened. Then she uttered a wailing cry and fell back dead into the pool and the water where she sank was dyed red with her blood.

'I have committed a wicked deed,' said Tristram Bird, gazing into the blood-stained pool, 'and it is certain that I shall be punished for my sin.' And he turned away with the fear of coming doom in his heart.

As he went up the cove and along the top of the cliffs the distressful, wailing cry of the Mermaid seemed to follow him and the sky darkened all around as he went and the sea moaned a dreadful moan as it came up the bay.

When he reached Tregirls, overlooking the Cove, he stood by the gate for a minute and gazed out over the beautiful harbour. The sea, which only half an hour ago was as blue as the eyes of the sea-maid he had shot and full of smiles and laughter, was now black as ash-buds, except where a golden streak lay across the water from Hawker's Cove to Trebetherick Bay.

'The Mermaid's curse is already working,' moaned Tristram Bird and he fled through the lane leading to Padstow as if a death-hound was after him. When he reached Place House he met a little crowd of Padstow maids going out flower-gathering.

'Where are you going so fast, Tristram Bird?' asked a little maid. 'You aren't driving a team of snails this time, 'tis plain to see. Where have you been?'

'Need you ask?' said a cheeky young girl. 'He has been away shooting something to startle the maids of Padstow with! What strange new creature did you shoot, Tristram Bird?'

'A wonderful creature with eyes like blue fire,' answered the unhappy young man, looking away over St. Minver dunes towards the Tors. 'A sweet, soft creature with beautiful hair, every wire of which was a sunbeam of gold and her face was the loveliest I ever saw. It clean bewitched me.'

'A beautiful maid like that and yet you shot her?' cried all the young maids of Padstow Town.

'Yes, I shot her, to my undoing and the undoing of our fair haven,' groaned Tristram Bird and he told them all about it: where he had seen the beautiful Mermaid, of his bewitchment from the moment he saw her face of haunting charm looking up at him from the Mermaid's Glass and of the curse she uttered before she fell back dead into the pool.

All the smiles went out of the bright faces of the Padstow maids, as he told his tale.

'What a pity, Tristram Bird, you should have been so foolish as to shoot a Mermaid!' they said and they did not go and pick flowers as they had intended but went back to their homes instead. Tristram Bird went on to Higher St. Saviour's, where he lived in his little house overlooking Padstow Town nestling like a bird in its nest.

A fearful gale blew on the night of the day Tristram Bird shot the Mermaid and all the next day, too and the next night and through the awful howling of the gale was heard the bellowing of the wind-tormented sea.

Such a terrible storm had never been known at Padstow Town within the memory of man, so the old men said and never a gale lasted so long. When the wind went down the natives of Padstow ventured out to see what damage the gale had done. Some went out to Chapel Stile, where a small chapel stood over-looking the haven and what should meet their horrified gaze but a terrible bar of sand which the Mermaid's curse had brought there. It stretched from Hawker's Cove to the opposite shore and what was worse, the great sand-bar was covered with wrecks of ships and bodies of drowned men.

'It is the bar of doom brought there by the fearful curse of the maid of the sea whom I shot with my brand-new gun,' cried Tristram Bird, who was one of the first to reach the stile when the wind had gone down; and he told them all, as he had told the Padstow maids, of what the Mermaid had said before and after he had shot her. 'And because of the wicked deed I did,' he said, 'I have brought a curse on my native town and Padstow will never be blessed with a safe and beautiful harbour till the poor Mermaid's death be avenged.'

There was a dreadful silence after Tristram Bird had spoken and the men and women of Padstow Town gazed at each other, troubled and sad. The wind was quiet, but the sea was still breaking and roaring on the back of the Doombar and as the waves thundered and broke a wailing cry sounded forth, like the wail that Tristram heard when the Mermaid disappeared under the water. All who heard it shivered and shook and both old and young looked down on the Doombar with dread in their eyes, but they saw nothing but the dead bodies of the sailors and their broken ships.

'It is the Mermaid's ghost,' cried an old man, leaning against the grey walls of the ancient chapel, 'and she is wailing the wail of the drowned; and, mark my words, everyone,' letting his eyes wander from one face to another, 'each time a ship is caught on this dreadful bar and lives are lost - as lost they will be - the Mermaid's ghost will wail for the drowned.'

And it came to pass as the old man said and whenever vessels are wrecked on that fateful bar of sand lying across the mouth of Padstow Harbour and men are drowned, it is told that the Mermaid's distressful cry is still heard wailing for the poor dead sailors.

THE LITTLE WHITE HARE

WHEN our great-great-grandmothers were young, a small lad called William John Pendarvey went on a visit to his Great-Aunt Ann, a very silent, austere old maid, who lived by herself in the Vale beautiful of Lanherne.

Great-Aunt Ann being old and very quiet, was the last person in the world that a tender-hearted, sensitive little chap as William John was should have gone to stay with.

The house where she lived was rather small and very gloomy, and had nothing nice about it, but it possessed a large and beautiful orchard, protected from the rough and cutting winds by the escarpment of the downs that rose above it and the valley.

But delightful as this orchard was, nobody except Great-Aunt Ann and she not often ever went into it, because it was known to be haunted by something, in the shape of a little White Hare which had been seen there from time unknown, wandering like a shadow over the grass, and in and out amongst the trees, or sitting motionless at the foot of a blasted apple-tree.

Who or what this apparition was nobody could tell, but not a man, woman or child in the Vale, except Great-Aunt Ann, would have gone into that orchard for all they were worth.

Little William John might never have known there was an orchard belonging to the gloomy old house if he had not wandered into a bedroom at the back of the house overlooking the entrance to the orchard and peeped out of the window.

He asked to be allowed to go and play there, as it looked so bright and sunny in its open spaces, but Great-Aunt Ann said: 'Not to-day.'

It was always 'Not to-day' whenever he asked to go into that orchard, and probably he would never have gone into it at all if the old maid had not occasion one day to go to St. Columb, a small market town three miles from where she lived. She could not take the boy with her, she said, and so she left him at home to take care of the house.

Looking after a house was not in little William John's line, and Great-Aunt Ann had not been gone more than an hour before he found himself at the small wicket-gate opening into the orchard, where to his joy he saw a great multitude of golden-headed daffadillies rising out of the lowly grass, and a light that was softer than silver moving mysteriously in and out amongst the trees. The temptation to go into that sun-lighted, fascinating spot was irresistible, and finding the gate unlocked, little William John opened it and went in.

It was the spring of the year, and the spring was late, and there were as yet no carmine buds on the apple trees, but their upper branches were misty with the silvery green of budding leaves. And the pear trees were in virgin whiteness, and so were the plum and cherry trees, which made a shining background to all the yellow lilies in blossom there.

'It makes me feel happy just to be here,' whispered little William John to himself; 'and the daffies are making golden dawns under the trees!'

He wandered about to his heart's content, staying his young feet now and then to listen to a blackbird's liquid pipe, and to touch with reverent hand a daffadilly's drooping head, or to watch with puzzled eyes that thing of brightness moving on in front of him amongst the trees and blossoms.

He lost sight of this wandering light when he had gone the length of the orchard; but he saw it again as he turned across to its top, and when he got close he saw, to his astonishment, it was a little Hare of silvery whiteness. It was sitting on its haunches under the blasted tree, and did not move away as the boy drew near.

A thrill of gladness filled William John's kind young heart at so fair and strange a vision, and his delight was even greater when the small White Hare suffered him to stroke its fur.

'Oh, you dear little soft thing!' he cried. 'I am so glad you are not afraid of me; I love all animals, and would not hurt any of them for worlds, nor a hair of your beautiful white coat.'

'I knew you would not,' answered the little White Hare. 'I was sure your heart was gentle and good the moment I saw you.'

'What! Can you talk?' asked little William John in amazement. 'I never knew animals could speak like human beings before. I am so glad you can. It is so nice to have someone to talk to. Nobody hardly ever speaks to me here, and I have felt so lonely.'

'Poor boy!' said the little White Hare; 'I can sympathize with you, for I know what it is to be lonely and have nobody to speak to. You are the first human being who has spoken to me since a wicked Witch turned me into the shape of a hare.'

'What! Are you not really a hare?' asked little William John, more and more amazed.

'No,' answered the little creature sadly; 'I am a maiden in the shape of a hare, and I have had to bear the hare-shape ever since the Witch worked a spell upon me, which was back in the days of the giants.'

'What a shame!' cried the boy. 'Whatever made her turn you into a hare?'

'She had a spite against me because I would not be wicked like herself.'

'How dreadful of her!' cried little William John indignantly. 'Will you never be able to get back your real shape, you poor little thing?'

'I am afraid not,' said the little White Hare sadly, 'unless somebody who is really sorry for me, and is not afraid of me, can find the Magic Horn by the blast of which Jack the Giant-

Killer over-threw the Giant Galligantus and Hocus-Pocus the Conjurer and blow over me three strong, clear blasts.'

'Where is the Magic Horn?' asked little William John.

'I do not know the exact spot, but it is buried somewhere in the ruins of an old castle called the Castle of Porthmeor, which is on a cliff above Porthmeor Cove.'

'Why, that old castle is mine, or will be, I am told, when I am of age!' cried little William John. 'It is not a great way from where I live, and often I go there to play. I wish I wasn't only a little boy, and could look for the Magic Horn,' he added, after a moment's silence.

'Age is no barrier to your seeking it,' said the little White Hare. 'All that is needed to loosen the wicked old Witch's spell is what I have now told you.'

'Then I will look for the Magic Horn directly I get home,' cried little William John, 'and if I can find it I'll come back and blow it over you, if you think I can.'

'I am sure you can,' answered the little White Hare. ' You must go now, for your Great-Aunt is coining into the valley. It is not wrong to come into this orchard, since she has not forbidden you; but she knows it is haunted by a little White Hare, and is afraid if you see it it will work you harm. So you must be patient with her.'

The Hare vanished as it spoke, and little William John found himself alone with the yellow-headed daffadillies, and the trees and dear little birds, and he soon went back to the house.

'Have you been out anywhere?' asked Great-Aunt Ann, when she had come in and taken off her bonnet.

'Yes, into the orchard,' said the boy truthfully. 'It is a lovely place, full of song-birds and flowers.'

'Was that all you saw there?' she asked anxiously.

'No,' answered little William John again, lifting his clear child-eyes to the stern old maid's. 'I saw trees with snow on them, and a dear little Hare with fur as white as milk.'

The old lady shook all over like a wind-tossed leaf when he said that, but she did not scold him or say he ought not to have gone into her orchard, but the next day she sent him home.

At the end of three years William John came again to stay with his Great-Aunt Ann - not that she wanted him, but because his guardian thought the balmy air of the lovely Vale would do him good.

The spring was very early this year, and when William John arrived the daffadillies had gone, and the pear and cherry trees had scattered all their snow-white blossoms on the grass; but the apple flowers were out in rosy splendour on the gnarled old trees, and where the daffadillies had made 'golden dawns' there were blue-grey periwinkles trying to lift themselves to the heavenly blue shining down upon them.

William John was anxious to go out into the orchard directly he came, but Great-Aunt Ann said the grass was too wet.

The grass was always 'too wet,' according to the old maid, and the boy was afraid she would not allow him to go into the orchard at all.

When he had been there two weeks and a day, Great-Aunt Ann had again occasion to go to St. Columb town, and as there was only room in the gig for the driver and herself, she was obliged to leave him at home.

The moment the gig was out of sight William John made his way to the orchard, where he found the grass as green and beautiful as spring grass could be, and his little friend the Hare sitting under the blasted tree, whiter and smaller than ever.

'I began to fear you would never come into this orchard again,' said the White Hare plaintively.

'I began to fear so myself,' responded William John, stroking very gently the little White Hare. 'This is my first opportunity of coming here.'

'Have you found the Magic Horn?' the small creature asked anxiously.

'Not yet, and I have never stopped looking for it since I was last here. I have searched all over the old castle, and every stone has been lifted on the place, and the ground dug up both outside the ruins and inside, and I am afraid the Magic Horn was not hidden away in that old castle, as you said.'

'It was hidden there, and is there now,' insisted the little White Hare, 'and I do hope you aren't going to give up looking for it.'

'I won't, for your sake, you dear little soft thing!' cried the boy, and again he stroked her gently and tenderly; 'and as you are sure it is there somewhere, I'll search until I find it.'

'Have you looked in the cave under the castle?' asked the little White Hare.

'No,' returned William John; 'the entrance to it is not known, and even if it were, the passage leading down to the cave is so foul with bad air, my guardian said, that it would be death to anybody who went through it.'

'If you are not afraid to go down into the cave, I can give you a plant that will purify all the foul air you pass through.'

'I will not be afraid for your sake, dear little White Hare,' said the boy.

The Hare vanished, and in a little while became visible again, and in her mouth she held a strange-looking weed, the like of which he had never seen before.

'It is called the little All-Pure,' said the White Hare, as William John took it in his hand. 'Keep it close to your heart until you have discovered the passage to the cave, and when it is foul hold it in your hand until its brightness shines on the Magic Horn.'

Again she disappeared, and the boy, after waiting some time to see if she would appear again, went back to the house, where he found his Great-Aunt Ann limping in at the front-door.

The old lady had hurt her leg in getting out of the gig, and when he told her he had been in the orchard, she made her slight accident an excuse to send him back to his home, which she did that same day.

William John did not have the chance of paying another visit to his Great-Aunt Ann until he was a youth of nineteen, and he would not have come then if he had waited to be invited.

The old maid was now terribly old and feeble, and had to keep a servant. Unhappily for William John, the servant was quite as crabbed and silent as her mistress, and even more opposed to his going into the old orchard. She even locked the orchard-gate and kept the key in her pocket.

But William John, being now no longer a child, but a handsome youth with a strong will of his own, was determined to get into the orchard with or without permission, for he had found the Magic Horn.

He watched his opportunity, and one day when the servant was out he went to the wicket gate and sprang over it, and quickly made his way to the blasted tree, where he found, as he had expected to find, the little White Hare sitting on her haunches under it.

She was very white and ever so small so small, in fact, that she did not look much bigger than a baby hare.

'You have come at last,' she said, as the tall handsome lad knelt on the grass and caressed her. 'Have you found the Magic Horn ?'

'I have found it,' he answered gladly.

'When did you find it ?'

'Only yesterday,' returned the youth. 'Every day since I last saw you I have searched for the entrance to the cave, and at last, when I was in despair of ever finding it, I came upon it under my bedroom window. I discovered it quite by accident, as I was planting maiden-blush rose-trees. I never knew till then that our house was built on the old castle grounds. The passage opened on to steps, which led down and down till they ended at the door of the cave.'

'Were you not afraid?' asked the little White Hare very softly.

'I was a little bit,' confessed the youth, 'for I did not know where it would lead me. But love and pity for poor little you made me go on. And I had the little All-Pure to cheer me; for it not only made the foul air through which I passed pure and sweet, but gave out a soft clear light. I found the Magic Horn on a slab of stone in the corner of the cave. I took it up quickly and returned the way I came, and started the earliest moment to pay a visit to my Great-Aunt Ann.'

'Have you brought the Magic Horn with you?' asked the little White Hare, with deep anxiety in her voice.

'Yes,' he said, with shining eyes, 'and here it is!' And he laid a black thing in the shape of a horn on the grass beside her.

'It is the Magic Horn,' cried the little White Hare joyfully. 'Will you blow over me three strong, clear blasts, dear William John? If you are as pure-hearted as you are kind-hearted, as I am sure you are, the last blast will break the Witch's spell, and give me back my own shape. The Horn should be blown at sunset.'

'It is sundown now,' said William John, looking westward, where between the trees he could see a splendour of rose and gold painted on the lower sky.

'Then blow it now!' cried the little White Hare; and stiffening herself on her form, she crossed her paws on her breast and waited.

William John took up the Magic Horn in his strong young hands and put it to his mouth, and in a minute or less there sounded out through the orchard, all gay with apple-blossom and melody of birds, and over the Vale of Lanherne, a great blast, so rich in sound that the thrushes stopped their singing, and the people in St. Mawgan village came rushing to their doors to know whatever it was. It was quickly followed by two more blasts, richer and louder than the first. When the last blast had died away, William John, looking down at the foot of the blasted tree, saw in the place of the little White Hare the most beautiful maiden he had ever seen.

The Magic Horn fell from his hand at so lovely a sight, and he blushed red as the buds clinging in rosy infancy to the apple-trees, and stammered something out that he had not expected to see her half so beautiful.

'I am myself now, thanks to you,' laughed the maiden; and William John thought it was the sweetest laugh he had ever heard in all his life. 'I can never be sufficiently grateful for all you have done for me.'

'Mine is the gratitude for having been allowed to find the Magic Horn and loosen you from the wicked spell,' said the lad, still stammering and blushing.

'You are very good to say so,' said the lovely maid, blushing in her turn as she felt the gaze of the handsome youth upon her. 'Now the evil spell has been undone I must go my way.'

'What way?' asked William John eagerly, drinking in the beauty of her face.

'To a country beyond the sun-setting, where all who love me are,' she said gently.

'If you go, I must also go,' said William John in a masterful way, still keeping his eyes on her face. 'I learnt to love you in your hare-shape, dear, but I love you a thousand times more now I see you as you are. I could not live without you now.'

'If you love me as you say you do, and cannot live without me, you may come,' said the lovely maid, lifting her shy eyes to his. 'You have the right to come with me by the good you have done. It is a fair land where I am going, where there are always buds and blossoms on the trees, where the happy birds are always in song, and where the Foot of Evil dare not enter. It is time I was away. The sun is setting, and his path of glory is narrowing on the sea. Come, if you will. I love you, too, dear.'

And giving him her little hand, which he gladly took, they went out of the old orchard in the glow of the setting sun. As they climbed a slope above the place of blossoming trees, an old man crossing the downs wondered who that handsome youth and lovely maid were making their way with locked hands and steadfast faces towards the sunset. But he never knew.

From that day onwards the little White Hare was never again seen in the old beautiful orchard, and nobody ever knew what had become of William John.

THE WITCH IN THE WELL

ONCE upon a time seven little maids of Padstow Town met together in Beck Lane to play a game called ' The Witch in the Well.' As they stood waiting for the child who was to act the witch, an old woman dressed in a steeple hat and chintz petticoat came down the lane towards them.

'What are you doing here, my pretty maids?' she asked.

'Waiting for our witch,' answered the children, wondering who this strange-looking, oddly-dressed old woman could be. 'We are going to play "Witch in the Well."'

'Are you?' said the queer old body. 'I used to play that nice game when I was young like you and should love to play it once again before I die. The little maid who was to have been your witch tumbled down on the cobble-stones in the market-place and hurt herself as she was coming hither,' she added, as they stared at her in amazement, 'and won't be able to play with you to-day. Will you let me be your witch instead of your little friend?'

'If you like, ma'am,' answered one of the children, after a hasty glance at her companions for consent.

'Thank you,' cried the old woman. 'It will be the most exciting game you ever played in all your life,' and, lifting her petticoats as if to display her high-heeled shoes and red stockings, she hobbled across the road to a well under a Gothic arch.

When the old crone had taken her seat inside the ancient well and which was called the Witch's Well Betty, the child who was to play the Mother in the game, took the other six little maids to a tumble-down cottage opposite the well and the game began.

The Little Mother told her children, who were called after the six working days of the week, that she was going down to

Padstow Town to sell her eggs and that they must not leave the cottage, as the Witch o' the Well was about.

'Mind the old witch doesn't come and carry you away,' the wee maids said one to another when the Little Mother had gone.

As they were saying this, the old woman in the chintz petticoat and steeple-hat came to the door and looked over the hatch.

'May I come in and light my pipe?' she asked.

'Yes, ma'am,' said Tuesday, unfastening the hatch; and when the old crone had come in and lighted her pipe, she crooked her lean old arm round Monday and took her away.

'Where is Monday?' asked the Little Mother when she had come back to her cottage, quick to see that one of her children was gone.

'An old woman came to light her pipe and took her away,' said Tuesday.

'It was the old Witch o' the Well,' cried the Little Mother. 'I'll go and see what she has done with her.'

Across the road to the well she went, and, stooping down and looking in, she saw an old woman sitting in the back of the well smoking a pipe.

'Where is my little maid Monday?' she demanded sternly.

'I gave her a piece of saffron cake and sent her to Chapel Stile to see if the waves were breaking on the Doombar,' answered the witch, knocking the ashes out of her pipe.

'I am off to Chapel Stile to look for Monday,' said the Little Mother, returning to the cottage. 'Be sure you don't let the old witch come in whilst I am away.'

Betty's back was no sooner turned than the same old woman came to the door.

'May I come in and light my pipe?' she asked.

'Yes, if you please, ma'am,' said Tuesday, forgetting her mother's injunction.

The old crone came in, lighted her pipe and took away Tuesday!

'Mind the old Witch o' the Well don't come and take you away like she did Monday and Tuesday,' the children were saying to each other when Betty came back from her fruitless search for Monday.

'What! has the bad old witch come and taken away Tuesday?' cried the Little Mother. 'Dear! whatever shall I do now? I can't find Monday and now my poor little Tuesday is gone!'

She rushed across the road to the well where the old witch was sitting, as before, calmly smoking her pipe.

'What have you done with Tuesday?' she demanded.

'I gave her a piece of saffron cake and sent her out to Lelizzick to ask Farmer Chapman to sell me a bag of sheep's wool for spinning,' the witch made answer.

'I am going out to Lelizzick to look for Tuesday,' said the Little Mother, rushing back to her children.

'Be sure you don't let the old witch come in. If you do, she will take you all away and then what shall I do without my dear little maids?'

Betty was scarcely out of sight when a steeplehat was seen at the window and a pair of eerie eyes looked in.

Before the children could shut the door and its hatch, the old witch had come into the cottage.

'A puff of wind blew out my pipe,' she said.

'May I light it with a twig from your fire?'

'Yes,' answered Wednesday somewhat doubtfully. 'But Mother told us we were not to let you come in, because, if we did, you would take us away as you did Monday and Tuesday.'

'Did she?' cackled the witch, taking a bit of stick from the fire and thrusting it into her pipe. 'Well, I only want one of you now,' and looking round the room, her glance fell on Wednesday and crooking her arm round her, she carried her off to the well.

'I have been out to Lelizzick and can't find Tuesday,' cried the Little Mother, coming into the cottage as the witch, with Wednesday under her arm, disappeared into the well. 'Oh!

where is Wednesday?' looking round the room and seeing another of her children missing.

'The old witch came in before we could shut the door and took our little sister away,' said the children.

'This is sad news, sure enough,' wailed the Little Mother and off she rushed to the well, where the witch was sitting smoking.

'What have you been and done with Wednesday?' she asked angrily.

'I gave her a bit of figgy-pudding and sent her to Place House to ask if Squire Prideaux's housekeeper would kindly give an old body a bottle of their good physic to cure her rheumatics.'

'I'm going up to Place House to see if Wednesday is there,' said the Little Mother, looking in at the window of the cottage. 'If the witch should come to the door whilst I am away, don't let her come in, whatever you do!'

When she had gone to Place House, an old mansion standing above Padstow Town, the old witch left the well and before the children saw her, she had pushed open the door and stood in the doorway, looking in.

'May I come in and light my pipe?' she asked.

'No,' answered Thursday.

But she came in, nevertheless, and having lighted her pipe, she caught up Thursday and took her across to the well.

'What! has the witch been here again and taken away Thursday?' exclaimed the Little Mother when she came back from Place House without finding Wednesday, discovering that another of her children was gone.

'Yes,' sighed Friday. 'She came over the doorsill before we saw her.'

'This is too dreadful!' cried the poor Little Mother. 'I shall soon have no little maids left to call my own!' and wringing her hands, she went across the lane to the well.

'What have you been and done with Thursday, you bad old witch?' she demanded.

'I gave her a piece of limpet-pie and sent her to London Churchtown to buy me a steeple-hat and a broom,' the witch made answer, rudely puffing her pipe in Betty's face. 'If you go there in Marrowbone Stage, you will perhaps find her.'

'I am off to London Churchtown in Marrowbone Stage to look for Thursday,' cried the Little Mother, returning to her cottage in great haste and excitement. 'Keep the door and hatch locked and barred till I come back, and then, if you are good children and do as I bid, I will bring you home each a gold ring.'

When the Little Mother had driven away in Marrowbone Stage to London Churchtown in search of Thursday, Friday saw the witch leave the well and cross the road to their cottage.

'Shut the door quickly and bar it,' she cried to Little Saturday.

And Saturday had but slipped the bolt into its socket when the old hag was at the door, knocking loudly to be let in.

'My pipe has gone out again,' she shrilled through the keyhole. 'May I come in and light it?'

'No!' answered Friday. 'Mother said you would take us away as you did poor Monday, Tuesday, Wednesday and Thursday, if we let you in.'

'I must come in and light my pipe,' insisted the witch. 'And if you don't open the door, I'll come through the keyhole.' As the children would not open the door, through the keyhole she came!

Having lighted her pipe and unbolted the door, she caught up both children and carried them away and when the tired Little Mother returned from London Churchtown in a fruitless search for Thursday, she found to her dismay not only Friday gone, but dear Little Saturday!

She hurried to the well in an agony of despair.

'Where is Friday and Little Saturday?' she cried.

'I gave them each a herby pasty and sent them to Windmill with grist to grind for to-morrow's baking,' answered the witch, spreading her petticoats over the dark water of the well.

'Tired as I am, I must go to Windmill to look for my dear children,' said the poor Little Mother, with a sigh. 'Perhaps I shall meet them coming back; and up the lane she went on her way out to Windmill.

When she came back to the well the old witch had smoked her pipe and was sound asleep and snoring.

'I have been all the way out to Windmill and I could not see Friday and Little Saturday anywhere,' cried the Little Mother, shaking the old hag roughly by the shoulder. 'Where are they, you wicked old witch?'

'Friday and Little Saturday came back soon after you had gone to look for them,' said the witch, opening her eyes and yawning.

'Where are they?' demanded the Little Mother.

'With Monday, Tuesday, Wednesday and Thursday,' answered the witch, knocking the ashes out of her pipe.

'And where is Monday and the others?'

'Upstairs,' answered the witch.

'Whose stairs?' asked Betty.

'My stairs,' returned the witch.

'Shall I go up your stairs and bring them?' asked the Little Mother eagerly.

'Your shoes are too dirty,' cried the witch.

'I will take off my shoes,' said Betty.

'Your stockings are too dirty/ protested the witch.

'I will take off my stockings.'

'Your feet are too dirty,' protested the old hag.

'I will wash my feet,' said the Little Mother.

'No water would wash them clean enough to climb up my stairs,' cried the witch.

'I'll cut off my feet,' persisted Betty, determined that no excuse should stop her from getting to her children.

'The blood would drop and stain my stairs,' said the witch.

'I'll tie up my stumps,' cried the Little Mother.

'The blood would come through,' howled the witch.

'Then, what shall I do to get up your stairs?' said the Little Mother, with a cry of despair.

'Fly up!' cackled the old hag.

'But I can't fly without wings,' wailed Betty.

'Get wings,' cried the witch, with a sneer.

'How can I?' asked the poor Little Mother helplessly.

'I leave that to your clever wits to find out!' snapped the witch. 'And let me tell you that until you can fly you will never see Monday and your five other children again, nor get them out of my clutches!' And with a 'Ha! ha!' and a 'He! he!' the witch pulled her petticoats round her and disappeared under the dark waters of the well.

'My dear life!' ejaculated Betty, now really frightened. 'I believe that old woman who played the game with us was a real witch and wasn't pretending at all and has really and truly taken Monday, Tuesday and all the others away.' And she sped away down to the quay where she lived with her terrible news.

There was a great to-do when the children's friends learned what had happened and there was bitter woe and lamentation when, after days and days of searching, the poor little souls could not be found.

*****

A year went by and all this time Betty, the child who had acted the "Mother" in the game, never forgot her six little friends. They were seldom out of her thoughts and she longed for a pair of wings to fly up the witch's stairs; and the more she wanted wings, the more impossible they seemed to get.

One evening in the beginning of June - the very same day, as it happened, that she and her little companions had met together at the Witch's Well to play the game - she was passing the well, when a little white dog ran out of a garden close by and came and licked her shoes.

She was fond of dogs and, as she patted it, to her amazement it began to talk to her just like a human being, which almost scared her out of her wits.

'Please don't be afraid of me,' he said, wagging his stump of a tail as Betty backed into the hedge. 'I am only a dog in shape. I was a little boy before the dreadful old Witch o' the Well turned me into a dog, or what looks like a dog.'

'Were you really a boy once? And do you know the Witch o' the Well?' asked Betty, trying to get over her fears in her interest in what he told her.

'Alas, I do!' answered the dog. 'She is my mistress and I have to follow her about all day long, and am never free of her except at night, when she is riding about on her broom. Then I have to haunt certain lanes to make silly superstitious people believe I am a ghost. The old Witch sent me to this lane a few days ago and very glad I was, because I hoped to see you.'

'Whatever for?' asked Betty, still very much afraid of this strange dog, with his human-like voice.

'Because I know your little friends Monday and the others.'

'Do you really?' cried the child. 'I am glad! Where are they?'

'In the witch's house, away on a dark moor, in her upstairs chamber,' answered the little white dog, with a wag of his tail, 'and where they will have to stay so the witch says until the little maid who played "Mother" in the game is able to fly upstairs after them.'

'Then, I'm afraid they will have to stay there always,' said Betty, her eyes filling with tears. 'Can't you get up the witch's stairs and bring them down?'

'The stairs are almost as steep as a tower,' answered the dog, 'and even if I could climb them, the door of the chamber where they are shut up is locked and a spell worked upon the lock that nothing can open save a pair of wings and music.'

'What kind of music?' asked Betty.

'I haven't the smallest idea,' answered the dog. 'I only know that it has to do with you.'

'Are my dear little friends happy?' asked Betty, hardly noticing the dog's last remark.

'They are most unhappy,' said the dog. 'They have nothing to cheer them, poor little souls, save the forlorn hope that perhaps one day their dear Little Mother Betty will be able to fly and get them out of the witch's power.'

'If I only knew how to fly, how quickly I would get up those stairs!' said Betty. 'There is nothing I can do, is there, to get a pair of wings?' she asked wistfully. 'Nobody who can help me to get wings?' she added, as the little white dog seemed to bend his head in thought.

'Nobody but the Wise Woman of Bogee Down,' he answered, after considering a few minutes.

'I have heard of that strange old body,' said Betty. 'My mother often told me about her. She is very clever and wise, she said and used to make medicines for sick people. She is terribly old now - a hundred and twenty, I think she told me.'

'That or more,' said the dog. 'But aged as she is, she is not too aged to work a kindness for anybody that asks her, particularly if it be against the Witch o' the Well.'

'Will she help me to get wings, do you think?' asked Betty eagerly.

'If it is within her power, I am certain she will,' returned the little white dog. 'Why don't you go and see her and tell her the old Witch o' the Well has shut up six dear little maids, who were unfortunate enough to play the game with her a year ago, and that they cannot be set free until you, who acted the "Mother" in the game, can fly up to their rescue?'

''Tis a long way to Bogee Down,' answered Betty, 'but I'll go there to-morrow, all the same, if I can.'

'That is well,' cried the little white dog. 'You will not seek her help in vain, I am sure, especially if you tell her the witch's little white dog Pincher sent you. Now I must be off, for the old witch is up on her broom and if she should happen to see us talking together, her horrid old cat would scratch our eyes out. Good-bye, dear little Betty and good luck with the Wise Woman.' With another wag of his tail he vanished.

Betty hardly slept a wink that night, thinking of her six little friends shut up in the witch's tower and so ardently did she desire wings to fly up to their help that she got up and dressed before the sun was risen. The sun was just rising on the east side of the river as she left her mother's house for Bogee Down, a wild, picturesque, but lonely place about four miles from the ancient town.

It was so early that nobody was up except herself, and the doors of the Crown and Anchor were still closed as she walked over the quay, down the slip, and across the beach to the south quay. The child went out of the town the nearest way to the downs, up through a side road called the Drang and up Sander's Hill. When she got up to Three Turnings, which commanded a view of the river and Padstow low in the hollow of the hills, she climbed a stile and looked down to see if she could see the quay.

The river was now very beautiful with reflections of the dawn and its pale-blue water was flushed with tenderest rose and gold. There was a flush on the rounded hills and a gleam of light on the distant tors - Rough Tor and Brown Willy. There was a ship in full sail coming up the harbour, followed by a company of white-breasted gulls, which also caught the light.

The sun was high in the sky when Betty reached Bogee Down. Now she had got there she did not know in what part of it the Wise Woman lived. As she sent her glance over the wild down, gorgeous with yellow broom and other down flowers, she thought she saw blue smoke rising from a hedge a short distance up from Music Water, a delightful spot where Sweet-Gales, Butterfly Orchises, Bog Asphodels grew and where a clear brown musical stream ran down between the fragrant flowers, which made the place that June morning very beautiful.

The child went up over the down where she had seen the smoke rising and found a hut huddled under a high blackberry hedge.

She knocked at the door, which was half open and a thin cracked voice called out: 'Come in and tell me what has brought you to this lonely down.'

Betty obeyed, but not without fear; and as she pushed the door open, she saw sitting in front of a peat fire on the hearthstone the bent form of an old woman with her back to the door. She was quaintly dressed, after the manner of ancient dames of the sixteenth century and on her head she wore a cap as white as sloe blossom.

The old dame did not look round as Betty entered, but when the child had said all that Pincher the little white dog had told her to say, and had asked if she would kindly help her to get wings to fly up the witch's stairs, she suddenly glanced at her over her shoulder, with the brightest, keenest eyes the girl had ever seen and which seemed to look into her pure young soul.

Evidently Betty's earnest little face pleased her, for she smiled and said kindly, 'Pincher was a wise dog to send you to me. But, let me tell you, you have asked me to do an almost impossible thing. Yet, fortunately for those poor shut-up little maids, it is not quite impossible; but it will depend on yourself, whether your love and pity for your little friends is strong enough to do all that is required of you.'

'I'll do anything if I can only get wings to fly with and see Monday, Tuesday and the others again,' broke in Betty, with all a child's eagerness.

'Alas! the will that is strong and eager to do is often weakened by the flesh that is frail,' said the Wise Woman, with a shake of her head, ' but the question now is, Are you willing to live with me, an old woman, in this out-of-the-way place, for a year and a day and do all I tell you willingly, without asking a single question?'

'A year and a day is a long time to be away from home,' said Betty honestly. 'Still, I am willing to stay with you all that time and do your bidding if my mother will let me.'

'That is well!' cried the Wise Woman. 'Now go back to Padstow Town and get your mother's consent and return to me to-morrow about this time.'

Betty's mother was very glad to let her little girl go and live with the Wise Woman, for she was very poor and had twelve children.

The next day, when Betty was returning to Bogee Down, which she did by the same road as before, with her clothes done up in a bundle under her arm, who should she see, leaning over a gate, at a place called Uncle Kit's Corner, but the old Witch o' the Well, smoking her pipe!

'Whither away, my little dear?' cried the witch, as the child drew near the gate.

'To get a pair of wings to fly up your stairs to see Monday and the others,' answered Betty promptly.

'Ha! ha! That's too funny!' cried the witch. 'You might as well try to cut a piece from the blue of the sky to make yourself a dress as to get wings to fly up my stairs.' And she laughed and laughed until she nearly choked herself.

'The witch may crow like an evil bird now,' cried the Wise Woman when Betty told her what the witch had said; 'but I shall hope to live to hear her screech like a weasel before that time has passed.'

When the little maid had undone her bundle, and put away her small belongings, the old woman told her to go to the settle, a long box-shaped wooden seat which stood by the fireplace, and take out from under its seat a little bag of feathers and separate one from the other and lay them on the table.

'That will be an easy thing to do,' said Betty to herself; and lifting the seat, she found a dinky bag stuffed full of feathers, rainbow-coloured, but so matted together that they were nothing but a soft ball.

'Perhaps this is to make me a pair of wings,' said Betty; and seating herself on the settle, she set to work with a will.

But the feathers were not easily disentangled, as she soon found and when evening came she had only succeeded in disentangling one tiny feather from the matted mass.

The Wise Woman neither looked nor spoke to her until the sun sank down behind the downs, when she told her to return the bag to its place in the settle and then get her supper and her own and go to bed.

'I have only got one little feather to put on the table,' said poor little Betty, when she had put the bag back into its place.

'You have done better than I feared,' said the Wise Woman quietly. 'It is something to have untangled even one feather from its companions. It is a sign that it is quite possible that you may be able to fly.'

When they had had their supper, which consisted of black bread and goat's milk, Betty lay down in a bed made of dried grass and bracken, in the corner of the room, and slept.

'It will take me a whole year to untangle all these feathers,' said the little maid to herself the next day, when she again sat down to her task, which she did when she had got her own and the Wise Woman's breakfast and had swept and sanded the hut. "It is dreary work, sure enough!'

'Pity, love and patience will do wonders,' said the Wise Woman, who seemed to have the gift of thought-reading and what she said comforted the child.

Every day for six long months Betty sat on the settle most of the day separating feather from feather and it was not until the end of that time that the last feather was laid upon the table. So bright and beautiful did they look that she said they looked as if they had been dipped in a rainbow.

The Wise Woman did not tell her what they were for, but she was sure they were to make her a pair of wings. 'And how beautiful they will be when they are made - brighter than a sunset!' she whispered to herself as she lay down to sleep that night.

When Betty awoke the following morning, she looked at the table to see if the feathers were safe and saw, to her dismay, the Wise Woman sweep them into the skirt of her gown and take them to the door and shake them out on the down.

'Oh, my beautiful feathers!' said Betty, springing up from her bed. But as she did so the ancient dame broke into a chant and all she could make out of it was that now the spell was broken they must go with all speed to the Queen of the Little People and get her permission to help in the undoing of another spell.

When the chant had ceased, Betty, still more amazed, saw a great cloud, that looked more like winged flowers than feathers, float away over the downs towards the sea.

'I don't believe they were feathers at all!' cried Betty to herself. 'And, oh dear! how am I to get my wings now?'

She longed to ask the Wise Woman to tell her why she had flung the feathers away, but remembering what the old body had said, that she was to ask no questions, whatever she saw or heard, she kept back the words on her lips.

When she had had her breakfast and had done all her little chores, the Wise Woman told her to search in the seat of the settle for a black stone, which, she told her, she must rub till it was the colour of life.

After much searching, she found a stone of curious shape wrapped in soft leather, which her old friend said she could use to rub the stone with.

Betty again set to work with a will, but rub as hard as she could, no rubbing seemed to affect the blackness of the stone and at the end of a week it seemed blacker than ever. She was much troubled at this, and the Wise Woman, who read her thoughts, told her not to despair, as its blacker blackness was a sign that all would be well, and that she was in a fair way of getting wings to fly up the witch's stairs.

'How?' was on Betty's lips, but a warning look from the Wise Woman's wonderful bright eyes made the question die unspoken.

For many a week longer the girl rubbed the sable stone patiently and quietly most of the time, but there were days when she felt like throwing the stone out of the window and running away home to her mother. But pity for her poor little friends shut up in the witch's chamber made her persevere with her task.

One day, when she was almost worn out with rubbing, she saw a faint glow come into the stone, which, as she rubbed harder and quicker than ever, grew brighter and brighter, until it lay in her hand as red as a poppy.

'The stone is all afire!' she cried, taking it to the Wise Woman.

'It is the colour of life at last,' said the ancient dame, gazing at it with her wonderful bright eyes; 'and another spell loosened to the witch's undoing,' she muttered, half to herself. And noticing that Betty was listening with all her ears, she told the child to look in the settle for a box and when she had found it to put it on the table and lay the stone within it.

There was only one box in the settle, which, though small, was most exquisitely carved all over with wings - wing interlacing wing - and as Betty set it on the table and put the stone into it, she thought she had never seen such a lovely box.

The next morning, when she awoke, she saw the Wise Woman at the door of the hut with the stone in her hand and she heard her chanting: 'Go the way thy sisters went - the way of the west wind and ask the King of the Wee Folk to give thee permission to help in the undoing of an evil wrought by the Witch o' the Well.'

Betty, staring with both eyes, saw the ancient dame fling the stone out on to the down, along which it rolled at a rapid rate, burning as it went with a rosy splendour. It went the way the feathers had gone.

Betty dressed quickly and busied herself about the hut, to keep herself from asking if the stone was really a stone, for she did not believe it was, and she ached to know.

When they had had breakfast, and the hut was cleaned with fresh scouring-sand, the Wise Woman asked her, if she had the chance of being made into a bird, what little bird would she like to be.

'A thrush,' said Betty. 'I should love to be a little thrush, because it sings so sweetly in the dawn.'

'It is a good choice,' cried the Wise Woman ' the best you could have made. Now go down to Trevillador Wood, and every thrush you see in it, ask him to give you a feather for Love's sake.'

'I do not know where Trevillador Wood is,' said the child, 'nor the way there.'

'It is in a valley in Little Petherick,' returned the Wise Woman. 'It is not a great way from here, and easy to find if you follow a little brown stream from Crackrattle, that runs down through the valley to the wood. Crackrattle is away there, on Trevibban Down,' pointing to the opposite down, which was only separated from Bogee by a narrow road. 'By going up across Trevibban you will soon get to Crackrattle. Now go, my dear and go quickly.' And Betty went.

The child was ever so thankful to be out of doors again, after having been cooped up in the hut for so many months, particularly as it was the birds' singing-time. Birds were singing everywhere on the downs and their music gushed from furze-brake, from thorn-bush and alder; and when she came to Music Water she heard linnets fluting and sweet wild notes came from budding willows by the side of the rippling stream. Larks were also singing, lark answering lark with such wonderful melody in the blue upper air that she told herself she had never heard such lovely sounds before.

The downs, in spite of all the bird-music, were not so beautiful nor so full of colour as when she came to stay with the Wise Woman. They were now as brown as Piskey-purses, she said and only lightened here and there by granite boulders, where they caught the rays of the sun, by yellow gorse and splashes of silver lichen.

It did not take the girl very long to cross Music Water's full stream to reach the road that parted the two downs; but it took her some time to get to Crackrattle, as the way up to it was thick with brambles and furze.

When she drew near that part of the down which commanded a grand view of the country and sea as far up as Tintagel, she turned her gaze towards Padstow Town and saw the river twisting in and out of the hills on its way out to the open sea. She also saw the two great headlands, Stepper Point and Pentire, that guarded the entrance to Padstow harbour in that far-away sixteenth century, as they do today and her glimpse of them and the blue river seemed to bring her home quite close to her; and when she reached Crackrattle stream, she followed it down the long, deep valley with a happy heart.

When she came to a wood, which she was sure in her mind was Trevillador Wood, she heard the thrushes singing and filling the place with music. Every cock thrush was doing his very best to out-sing his brother thrush. It was mating-time and each little songster in speckled grey was trying to win a little mate by his song.

The first thrush that Betty saw - and he was a master singer and made the wood ring - was on the uppermost branch of a horse-chestnut just beginning to bud and when he had finished his entrancing song, she lifted up her voice and said, 'Dear little grey thrush, please give me one of your feathers, for Love's sake.'

She wondered as she begged if the bird would understand her language; but he did quite well, and, what she thought was still more wonderful, she understood his!

'I will give you a feather gladly,' he piped in his own delicious thrush way. 'It is the beautiful spring-time and the thrushes' courting-time; and because you beg a feather for Love's sake, I will pluck one that lies over my heart.' And the dear little bird did so and flung it down into Betty's outstretched hands; and when she had caught it, he burst out into exquisite melody and he was still singing, as she went down the wood lovely with budding trees.

From every thrush she saw she asked a feather for Love's sake, and she was not refused once, and by the time she had gone the length of the wood her apron was full of thrushes' feathers, plucked from breast and wing, tail and back!

'Were the song-thrushes willing to give their feathers?' asked the Wise Woman when Betty got back to the hut.

'Ever so willing!' cried the little maid, opening her apron to show what a lot she had got.

'It is more than enough,' she said. 'Put them into the box where the stone lay.'

The following morning when the child awoke there was a mournful sound coming up from the sea, which they could hear from the door of the hut, and the Wise Woman said it was a sign that a great storm was being brewed by the Master of the Winds, and that before the day was over he would send the great North-Easterly wind across the land.

'I am sorry,' she said, 'as it will hinder our work and perhaps I shall die of the cold before we can help you to fly.'

Betty wanted terribly to ask the Wise Woman who beside herself would help her to get wings, but she dared not ask a single question and felt it was very hard she could not.

Before the day had closed in, the bitter north wind, which was accompanied by snow, had come. It broke over the downs in great fury and made the poor old woman shiver over her fire with the misery of it. The next day and the next it blew, and the more it blew and the faster it snowed, the more the ancient dame shivered and shook; and all day long she kept Betty busy piling up dry furze on the hearth, till there was none left.

When she realized that all her winter store of peat and firewood was burnt, she moaned and said she was sure she should die of the cold.

'And if I die,' she added sadly, 'the witch, like the north wind, will have it all her own way and you will never be able to fly up her terrible stairs.'

This distressed the poor little maid very much; for she had become quite fond of the Wise Woman and wanted her to live for her own sake as well as for Monday's, Tuesday's and the others'.

When the fuel was all burnt, and the Wise Woman too cold even to shiver, Betty said that when it stopped snowing she would go out on the downs and look for something to burn; and when it stopped she went.

The downs were many feet deep under the snow and there was not a furze-bush nor a hillock to be seen anywhere; and the down opposite was as smooth as a sheet spread out on grass to dry.

As Betty was searching for wood, and could not find even a stick, a hare came speeding over the snow from Crackrattle. She watched it till it crossed over to Bogee and saw, to her surprise, that it was making straight for her. When it drew near it stopped, with eyes that made her think of the witch's eyes, and as it gazed, the hare disappeared, and in its place stood the old witch herself, steeple-hat and all!

Betty was dreadfully frightened. But before she could rush back to the hut, the witch had come quite close to her and asked her what she was doing out there in the cold.

'Looking for firewood for the poor old Wise Woman's fire,' answered Betty. 'And I can't see any,' she added sadly.

'Of course you can't,' laughed the witch. 'Sticks under three feet of snow are as difficult to find as a furze-needle in a wagonload of hay. It will comfort you to know that you won't find even a stick and that before the north wind has turned his back on the downs, the Wise Woman will have died of the cold, and you will cry your eyes out for wings to fly up my stairs!' And cackling and jeering, she disappeared and Betty saw a gray hare running away over the snow down to Music Water, now as silent as the downs themselves.

The little maid was returning to the hut with an icicle of despair at her heart, when a white dog ran across her path and looking down, she saw it was Pincher, the witch's dog.

'Don't let what my bad old mistress said distress you,' he cried, licking Betty's cold little hand. 'She does not want you to look for sticks and came here on purpose to prevent you. She is quite as anxious that the Wise Woman should die as you and I are for her to live. She is as clever as she is vile and she knows that a woman over a hundred could not possibly live long in awful weather like this unless she has a good fire to keep her warm.'

'But why does she want the Wise Woman to die?' asked the little maid.

'Because she fears the wisdom of her long years can help you to fly up her stairs. And this fear brought her to Bogee Down to-day. She made me come with her, which is fortunate; for poking about whilst she was talking to you, I discovered a great faggot of wood dry as a bone and under it a pile of peat.'

'Where?' Betty asked eagerly.

'Close to the hut under a hedge,' answered the dog. 'And if you will allow me I'll come and help you to get it out. The witch is so happy in her belief that she has discouraged you from looking for sticks that she won't miss me yet.'

And he led the way to the side of the hut, where, under a tangle of brambles, Betty saw a huge bundle of sticks, dry and brown.

They set to work with a will, she with her eager young hands, he with his strong white teeth and soon got it out from under the hedge and into the hut, where, to their distress, they found the Wise Woman lying face down on the hearthstone, apparently lifeless.

Betty began to sob, believing the poor old woman was dead, which made Pincher quite angry and he told her with a growl to put off her weeping till a more convenient time, and see if she could not kindle a fire with the sticks they had brought, whilst he tried to lick life back into her poor old body.

It was just the stimulus the child wanted. She mopped away her tears and piled wood on the fire and set it alight; and Pincher, the dog, licked the poor old woman's face and hands with his warm, moist tongue.

Their efforts were not in vain and they soon had the joy of seeing her open her eyes and stretch out her hands to the blaze.

'Thank you for all your kindness, dear Pincher,' said Betty, when the dog said he must go. 'If I can ever do you a kindness in return, just ask me and I'll do it if I can.'

'Remember me when you can fly up the witch's stairs,' said the dog, with an appealing look in his eyes that Betty never forgot.

'Then you really believe I shall be able to fly up those stairs some day?' she asked.

'I am almost certain you will and so is the witch. You cannot live with people for generations without being able to read their faces. The witch's face is an open book to me now and it tells me that she is not only afraid you will fly, but that it will happen soon. So fearful is she of this that a few days ago she actually wove another spell on the door leading up to the tower where the little maids who played the game are kept.'

'Do you ever get to talk with the poor little dears?' asked Betty wistfully.

'Never. But I sometimes see them at the barred window of their chamber. It isn't often they have time even for that, for the old witch keeps them spinning all day long. Farewell, dear! I must go. If the faggot of sticks is all burnt and the turf before the cold goes, don't go out again in search of more firewood. There is danger abroad. If the Wise Woman is in danger of sinking under the cold, just lay your warm heart against her heart and all will be well.'

The dreadful weather still continued and when the faggot was all burnt, the dame again began to shiver and shake with cold, and said she should die this time, as there was no warmth left to keep life in her.

Betty was once more greatly distressed on her old friend's account and declared she would go out on the downs to look for firewood in spite of what might happen to herself; but as she was going, the Wise Woman again tumbled, face down, on the fireless hearth.

As the girl picked her up and laid her on the settle, she remembered what the dog had advised her to do if the cold overcame the old woman again and, lying down beside her, she pressed her warm young body against her aged body and soon she had the joy of knowing that life was creeping back to the feeble old frame.

When the Wise Woman opened her eyes and saw the child's face close to hers and felt her kind young arms about her, she said, with a tremble in her voice, 'You are a dear little maid. You have rekindled the feeble flame of my life, proving to me that Good is greater than Evil and Love stronger than Hate. I shall not die now before you have got your wings. Get up, open the door and call across the snow three times, "Little Prince Fire, come away from the Small People's Country and keep the Wise Woman warm till the cold goes!"'

Betty made haste to obey and when she had opened the hut-door wide she called three times, as she was told and then waited to see what would happen.

In a minute or less there appeared on the edge of the down a bright-red glow like a poppy in the eye of the sun. After burning there a minute or so it came like a flash over the snow towards the hut. As it came close, she saw it was the very same stone that she had rubbed for so many, many weeks.

It flashed like a ruby into the hut and as it did so she thought she saw, through the soft rosy haze that seemed to envelope it, a tiny laughing face.

When she turned to see where the stone had gone, she saw it was on the hearthstone, burning away like a tiny faggot, and the Wise Woman was sitting beside it with her withered old hands held out to the blaze!

It was so remarkable and queer that Betty could not at first believe the evidence of her own eyes and rubbed them to make sure she was not dreaming. But it was no dream, for the miserable little hut, which a few minutes before was cold as Greenland, was now as warm as an oven and there was a soft glow all over it.

She sat down on the settle to enjoy the comfort of this wonderful fire, and she felt so warm and lovely after the terrible cold that it made her drowsy, and in a little while she was in a sound sleep. She never knew how long she slept, she only knew that when she awoke the wind and the snow had all gone and the down birds were chanting a morning song outside the window. The stone was also gone and the Wise Woman nowhere to be seen.

As she was wondering what had become of her, the old woman came into the hut with her apron full of green furze and seeing the child wide awake, she cried, 'Get up, sleepyhead! The cold has left the downs and the thrushes in Trevillador Wood have built their nests and are beginning to lay. Hurry to the wood and get a bottleful of bird-music.'

'Where is the bottle?' asked Betty, getting up and looking about her.

'You will find one in the settle made of the Small People's crystal, into which you must ask every thrush you hear singing to his mate to drop a note to make a song with. Ask him to give it you for Gratitude's sake. When the bottle is full to its neck make your way back to the hut and the first living thing you see after you have left the wood ask it to return with you to the Wise Woman. Ask it also to come for Gratitude's sake.'

After the child had eaten some food and had found the bottle, which was ever so tiny, and clear and bright as diamonds, she started for Trevillador Wood.

The cold had indeed all gone, as the Wise Woman had said and the downs were all the better for the great storm that had swept over them. The snow had kept the earth warm, and had been a soft warm blanket to all the flowers, and now the furze blossom was all manner of lovely shades of gold and the soft spring air full of its fragrance. Music Water was all alight with marsh-marigolds and the catkins of the grey-green willows were dusted with gold.

The snow had also been kind to the trees in Trevillador Wood (the Thrushes' Wood, Betty called it) and had wrapped all the baby buds and tender leaves in dainty white furs. When the little maid entered the wood she saw, to her surprise, that most of the trees were dreams of beauty, with glistering leaves, and some of them were almost as brightly coloured as that strange stone, Little Prince Fire, as the Wise Woman had called it.

So delighted was she with all she saw that she forgot what she had been sent there for, until a thrush near startled the wood with a burst of melody. He was singing to his mate, for, drawing nearer, she saw, low down in a bush, a little hen thrush on her nest.

'Please, little song-thrush will you drop a note of your song into this bottle for Gratitude's sake?' she asked, holding up the bottle to the singing thrush.

'Gladly,' piped he, 'especially as you ask it for Gratitude's sake. We have just received our first great blessing, which I may tell you is a tiny blue egg.'

'Give the child two notes,' piped a happy little voice from the nest. 'My heart is brimming over with joy for the warm little thing under me.'

'Thank you for your kindness,' said Betty. 'But, if you please, little thrushes, the Wise Woman who lives on Bogee Down above Music Water, who sent me to this wood, said I must only ask for one note from each thrush I heard singing.'

'That is right,' chirped the little cock thrush. 'Always obey those older and wiser than yourself.'

'Ask the child what she wants thrushes' notes for,' chirped the voice from the nest. 'She didn't say, did she?'

'I forgot to tell you that,' struck in Betty. 'It is to make a song with.'

'I thought so,' piped the little cock thrush and flying down, he put one of his most delicious notes into the tiny bottle, and in another second he was up on his bush again, singing deeper and more entrancingly than before, gratitude being the keynote and the chief utterance of his song.

Betty went down the wood with that music in her soul and begged every thrush she heard singing to give her a note of his song.

Whether every bird's heart was also full of gladness for the freckled blue eggs in its dear little nest we cannot say, but they all gave willingly of their best, and before the child had gone through Trevillador Wood, the bottle of Small People's crystal was full to the neck with thrush-music.

Coming back, she saw two red squirrels sitting on their haunches at the foot of an oak-tree, eating nuts.

Said one squirrel to the other squirrel, 'There is a dear little maid from Padstow Town here in the wood collecting music from the thrushes. It is the same child who, unknown to herself, undid a cruel spell which the Witch o' the Well cast over Prince Fire, a near relative of the King of the Little People. She turned him into a black stone and a stone he had to be till somebody could rub it the colour of flame.'

'You don't mean to say so?' cried the other squirrel. 'This is news.'

'I thought it would be,' said the squirrel that spoke, arching his handsome tail with importance. 'Perhaps it will also be news to you to hear that this same little maid has actually untangled the dear Little Lady Soft Winds from that great Skein of Entanglement into which the wicked old witch tangled them and from which nobody, not even the Wee Folk themselves, was able to free them.'

'However did she manage to do it?' asked the second squirrel.

'Only the Wise Woman of Bogee Down could answer that question. But the thrushes believe, and so do I, that love and pity for six little maids whom the witch has shut up somewhere gave patience to her fingers to do what the Wise Woman bade her do; and because her heart was full of love for these poor little maids, whom she hoped by her obedience to get out of the witch's power, she unwittingly set free the other poor little prisoners the Lady Soft Winds and Prince Fire, the King's cousin.'

'And has she got her own little friends out of the power of the witch after all her love and patience?' asked the squirrel.

'Alas! not yet; but we all hope she will soon. The Small People are her friends now, especially those she set free. And it is told that they are going to turn her into a flying creature of some sort. Some say a bird, but nobody knows for certain. We are all on the alert to see what will happen. They say the Lady Soft Winds whispered to the daffodowndillies last evening that Prince Fire had already begun to make a pair of wings for her to fly up the witch's stairs. But it may be only talk. And yet - there! The dear little maid is coming. Not another word, remember. She understands our language and bird language too. The Wise Woman, it is said, put something on her tongue when she was asleep one day, when Little Prince Fire came from the Wee Folk's country to keep the Wise Woman's hut warm;' and then, catching sight of Betty's eyes bent upon him, he rushed up the trunk of the oak, followed by his companion.

'Well, those little funny things have told news, sure enough,' laughed the child to herself when the pretty little squirrels had vanished, 'and have told me all I ached to know without asking a single question. To think that the little feathers were the dear Little People; and that queer black stone was one too and that they are going to help me fly up to Monday and the rest!'

And she danced with delight as she thought of it and the wonder was she did not dance the thrushes' notes out of the bottle.

When she was out of the wood, and walking up to Crackrattle, she remembered what the Wise Woman had told her, that she must ask the first living thing she saw to return with her to the hut; but the only creature that she noticed as she went up the valley was a large butterfly - or what she thought was a butterfly - on a great stone.

'The Wise Woman cannot want a butterfly to go back with me to her house,' said Betty to herself. 'But perhaps I had better ask it to come;' and speaking gently, so as not to frighten away the lovely thing on the stone, she said: 'Little butterfly, please will you, for Gratitude's sake, come with me to the Wise Woman's hut?' and to her amazement the tiny creature answered back :

'Gladly will I go with you. But, excuse me, I am not a butterfly. I am one of the Lady Soft Winds whom you freed from the tangle into which the old witch threw us.'

It began to rise on its azure wings as it spoke and as it rose Betty saw it was indeed a fairy. It had the dearest little face she had ever seen and as for its eyes, they were bluer than its own wings and its soft, round cheeks were a more delicate pink than the cross-leaved heath that flowered on the downs early in the summer.

It flew on beside her and Betty was so taken up with watching it that she did not notice when she got up to Crackrattle that a dozen other fairy-like creatures were flying over the downs towards her, until they were quite close.

'We are the Lady Soft Wind's sisters,' they said, 'and out of deep gratitude to you we have come to go with you to the Wise Woman's hut'

'Have you really, you little dears?' was all Betty could find words to say. 'Come along, then.' And they came and were a rhythm of colour as they flew beside her, or, as the child expressed it, 'a little flying garland of flowers.' Thus accompanied, Betty came to the hut, where, in the doorway, stood the Wise Woman, leaning on her stick, evidently awaiting her and her companions' arrival.

'We have come,' said one of the little creatures.

'I felt certain you would,' said the Wise Woman, making a curtsey, 'and a thousand welcomes. If the child has brought the thrushes' notes everything is ready.'

'She has brought them,' put in another tiny voice, 'and they are impatient to sing.'

'Then please follow me,' said the Wise Woman, going into the hut; and in flew all the lovely little creatures, with gentle fanning of wings, which made a soft breeze as they came.

'Prince Fire is already at work,' said the Wise Woman, pointing to the box, and Betty, who had followed the Little Lady Soft Wings, saw, sitting in the box amongst the thrushes' feathers, a small person dressed in red, busy making wings! He was Little Prince Fire and a very great person in the Small People's World.

'My dear life! Oh, my dear life! What shall I see next?' cried the little Padstow maid to herself; and what more she would have said is not known, for at that moment the Wise Woman took the tiny crystal bottle out of her hand and put it into the box beside the dinky person within.

'The Lady Soft Winds have arrived, your Royal Highness,' she said, 'and Betty, the little Padstow maid, is also here.'

'Good!' piped the tiny man. 'Bid them sing the Making Song.'

'We require no bidding, Prince Fire,' said a little Lady Soft Wind, with gentle dignity, as she and the others alighted on the table. 'Out of gratitude and love we have come from afar to sing this song, knowing well, unless we sang it, you would never complete the wings. We, as well as you, can never repay the little maid of Padstow Town for releasing us from the witch's spell.

The voice had hardly died away when all the radiant fairies began to wave their wings, at first slowly, and then rapidly, in a kind of rhythm, and sang very softly as they waved them.

Betty watched them with all her eyes and whether it was the movement of their wings or the curious song they sang, with its hush-a-by kind of tune, she felt ever so drowsy, just as she had felt when Little Prince Fire blazed away like a faggot on the hearthstone, and sitting down on the settle, she fell asleep with the two first verses of the song in her ears :

'We Wee Folk together
With music and feather
The gift of the birds-
The little grey-birds
Do make her a thrush
All sweetness and gush.
    Lallaby! Gallady!
'And the Little Prince Fire
Her sweet song will inspire,
That she may fly high
Where little maids sigh,
And undo the spell
Of the Witch o' the Well.
    Lallaby! Gallady!'

The next thing she heard was the Wise Woman telling her to rise up and move her wings and Betty lifted herself from the settle and found she was all air and lightness, like the Little Lady Soft Winds themselves, and could fly about the hut with the greatest ease. The feeling of flying was altogether delightful!

The Lady Soft Winds watched her flight with the deepest interest and Prince Fire, who was sitting on the edge of the carved box, watched too; that he approved of her flying powers it was plain to see, for his bright eyes never left her.

'What am I now?' asked Betty at last, perching on a beam and looking down sideways bird fashion on the Wise Woman.

'You are a little grey thrush,' said the Wise Woman, her withered face a big smile.

'And now, little grey thrush, away to the east, where the witch's house looms out dark and strong against the gold of the morning sky,' said the Lady Soft Winds, 'and fly up her terrible stairs and set your six little children free, as you did us.'

'Yes; away to Monday, Tuesday and Wednesday,' cried Little Prince Fire.

'And Thursday, Friday and Little Saturday,' struck in the Wise Woman.

'Away, away, little grey thrush!' cried they all, singing as they cried. 'The sun is rising behind the Tors and the time is come for our little thrush to fly and sing. Then, away, away!'

Their little thrush wanted no further urging and with one full, clear, melodious note, which filled all the small fairies with delight, it flew out of the hut, followed by the gentle winnowing of the Lady Soft Winds' wings.

So glad was Betty, the little grey thrush, at being on her way to see those dear little maids that she flew faster than ever a thrush flew before and the sun was not yet over the Tors when she reached a grim old house standing all alone on a brown and desolate moor, with its back to the golden sunrise.

Instinct told the little grey thrush that it was the witch's house and alighting on a blasted tree, close to its spell-bound door, she began to sing with all her might; and so joyous and so triumphant was her song that it seemed to bring gladness and hope even to that desolate spot.

As Betty, in her bird form, sang on, the old witch came round the corner of her house, dragging her unwilling feet as she came. When she lifted her bad old eyes and saw a grey thrush high on the tree, singing with all its cheerful heart, she turned green and hearing the door of the tower leading up the stairs where Monday and all the other little maids were shut up groaning as if in pain, she sank in a heap on the ground and began to groan and moan too.

The bird sang on, and its whole body shook with its music, and the more thrilling its song, the more the witch moaned and groaned. Then, when its last triumphant note rang out, the great door opened, as if pushed back by some magic power and revealed a flight of very steep stairs. The witch gave a piercing howl when she saw the door open wide, for she knew that the small grey thrush's music had broken her spells and that she was completely in the power of that little singing bird.

When the door of the tower was as wide open as it could go, the thrush gave three flaps of its wings, flew out of the tree and in through the doorway of the tower, up and up the witch's stairs. And at the top of the stairs was a small room, where six little maids sat spinning.

They were so busy and the hum of the wheels was so loud, that none of them noticed the entrance of the grey-bird until it broke into a song from the window-sill.

'Why, it is a dear little thrush!' cried Friday, who was the first to notice it. 'How ever did it get up here? It must be the bird we heard singing so beautifully outside just now,' and all the children stopped their spinning-wheels to look at it.

'Did it really fly up the witch's stairs?' asked Thursday, resting her sad, soft eyes on the thrush, whose heart was beating so against its speckled breast at the sight of those dear little maids that it couldn't tell them at first who it was.

'It did,' answered Monday, 'and its flying up here makes me think of our Little Mother Betty, who played the game with us. Will she ever be able to fly up the witch's stairs, I wonder?'

'I am afraid not,' said one of the other children, with a sigh. 'I have given up all hope of her ever doing that now.'

'You are wrong, my dears,' cried the thrush, finding its voice at last. 'I am Mother Betty, turned into a dinky bird for your sakes and have flown up the witch's stairs!'

And it flapped its wings, jerked its tail and behaved altogether in a most extraordinary manner, for the children's faces of amazement and hope nearly sent it mad with joy. And then, as if it must relieve its feelings still more, it burst into a most enchanting song, which was answered outside the tower by a series of joyful barks from Pincher, the witch's dog.

'It must be Little Mother Betty,' said Monday, leaving her spinning-wheel. 'I can hear her own voice in the song.'

Then all the other little maids left their wheels to gaze at the bird.

'Are you really Betty who played the " Witch in the Well " with us that terrible day?' they asked.

'Indeed I am,' sang the thrush. 'I have come to take you away from here. Now follow me down the stairs and out of the house.'

'The stairs are so steep,' began Saturday, with frightened eyes.

'Don't be afraid, dear little Saturday,' sang the bird. 'It will be as easy as thinking. Come along, all of you.'

The six little maids followed the bird out of the room and down those wall-like stairs and in a minute or less were outside the witch's house, where they found the old hag in the act of mounting her broom.

They were met at the door by Pincher the dog, who welcomed them with joyful barks and wagging of tail. Then, finding his mistress had fled, he looked up at the little grey thrush, who was wheeling round and round the children's heads out of sheer gladness, and begged her to give chase to the witch. 'For,' said he, 'if she goes out of your sight before you have commanded her to do something, you are in danger of having to retain your thrush-shape.'

'I am glad you told me,' said Betty and she was about to fly after the witch, when she recalled to mind what the dog had said the day he helped to drag the faggot of wood into the hut : 'Remember me when you have flown up the witch's stairs.'

'I have been up the witch's stairs and down again,' she said, alighting on the ground beside him. 'Is there anything I can do for you, Pincher? I am here to do it if I can.'

'I long to be set free from the power of the witch,' said the little dog, fixing his gentle eyes on the bird, 'and to be restored to my own shape. If you bid the witch do this, though it will be vinegar and gall to her, she is bound to obey you by the merit of your wings and your song. I long exceedingly to be myself again.'

'You shall,' sang the little grey thrush.

And then, telling the children to run and follow hard after her and the witch, she flapped her wings again and flew after the old hag on her broom and Pincher the dog and the six little maids sped after them.

Over the moor and across the downs they all went like the wind, the witch keeping well in advance. Uphill and downhill and through the lanes they flew and never once did they stop till they came to Place Hill, where the great stone gateway of Place House stood greyly out from a background of beech trees and oaks. Here the six little maids stopped to get breath, but the old hag, though ready to drop from her broom with fatigue, paused not a second and went on down the hill with little thrush Betty and Pincher the dog close behind her.

'The witch is out of sight!' cried Monday, as the old hag and the little grey-bird disappeared round a corner.

'So she is!' said Friday.

Away they sped down the steep hill in pursuit of the witch; but they did not overtake her until she got to the well, when they stood watching to see what would happen.

The old hag slid off her broom, and, looking cunningly about her, as if in search of the thrush, which was on top of the wall above the well, she made a quick step to the well, and put her foot on its ledge.

'Sing, sing, dear Thrush Betty!' cried the small white dog in great distress, or the witch will disappear into the well before you can command her to do what you said.'

And Betty, the little grey-bird, flew into a tree, and began to sing with all her might once more. And as she sang, the old hag crept back from the well, and stood in the middle of the road, with a terrible look on her face.

Now, being a witch, and one of the worst of her kind, she could not endure anything so pure and sweet as the small bird's song; every note it sang was an agony to listen to, and, knowing in her wicked soul that its music had crushed all her evil power, she begged permission in a humble voice to be allowed to go into the well.

'You may go,' sang little Thrush Betty; 'with one condition, which is that you turn Pincher back into a boy!'

'Please ask me something less hard!' pleaded the witch, cringing before the little bird. 'Pincher will be mine no longer if I do that and I cannot do without my faithful little dog. Where I go, he must also go.'

'That he shall not!' sang the thrush. 'I command you, by the merit of my wings and the power of my song, to remove your spell from this poor little boy!'

'To lose my little white dog is worse than having the Lady Soft Winds and Prince Fire set free from my spells!' muttered the witch. 'Worse even than losing the six little maids who played the game with me and did all my spinning.'

'Give him back his own self this very minute,' sang the little grey thrush, 'or else!'

If a threat was implied in the sentence, the witch understood it, for, with a howl of rage, she made a pass with her broom over the dog. As she did so, the dog vanished, and in its place stood a young boy, dark and very handsome, dressed in clothes of a bygone age!

The six little maids stared at him in open-mouthed astonishment and as they stared as only little maids can, the witch made for the well.

'Please sing once more, little Thrush Betty,' cried the boy in a voice she knew so well. 'This last song will quite end the power of the bad old witch and keep her down in the bottom of the Witch's Well until she repents of all she has done.'

'That will be never!' snarled the witch; and with a horrible cry, which even the victorious song of the little grey thrush could not drown, she splashed into the well. And when Monday, Tuesday and the other little maids could get that cry out of their ears, the well and its quaint old arch were no longer to be seen and near where it had stood was dear little Betty, their friend, who had played the "Mother" in the game, looking very little altered, only a few inches taller, and standing beside her, holding her hand, was the boy, who, in his dog-shape, had done so much for them all.

'Now let us go home to our mothers,' cried Friday.

'I have no mother to go to,' said the boy sadly, as he hesitated to go with the happy children. 'Mine died long ago and I have no home.'

'Our mothers shall be your mother,' cried the little maids, 'and you will never lack anything if you come with us.'

So they all came down through Padstow Town, the boy in their midst.

Nobody noticed them till they reached Middle Street, a straight cobbled street with quaint houses on either side, when a very old man spied them and shouted the news that the long-lost children had come back and the whole street rushed out to welcome them.

Thursday lived at the bottom of this street and Betty thought she ought to see her safely home; but the child's mother had already heard of their arrival and came out to meet them and to clasp her own little maid to her heart.

Monday's home was in a narrow street called Lanedwell and when she was safe within her parents' house and arms, the other five little maids and the handsome boy, accompanied by a great crowd, went on their way to the market, where Saturday lived.

As they came out of Lanedwell Street, a house across the market stood full in view. It was one of the quaintest of buildings, of Tudor date, with an outside flight of stone stairs leading up to its side entrance -under the eaves. Little Saturday's eyes glistened when she caught sight of this house, for it was her own dear home. Her father happened to be at the top of the stairs looking over the wooden rail as the children drew near and he nearly fell over into the street below when he saw his own long-lost little maid.

Through a narrow passage, called the Blind Entry, the children and crowd of people poured and they only got through when Saturday's father was down the steps and over to the Entry to greet them.

'There is the "George and the Dragon"!' cried Thursday, pointing to an inn at the bottom of a street as they crossed the market.

'Yes,' said Betty, with a smile; 'and St. George is still slaying the Dragon!' gazing up at the sign hanging above the door.

'Perhaps the Dragon is even more difficult to conquer than the Witch o' the Well,' put in the boy, eyeing with great interest the inn's sign, on which was painted in glowing colours England's patron saint, with uplifted sword to slay the Dragon.

'Ever so much more, I reckon,' responded Betty.

Another small street brought them to the quay, where the other four little maids' homes were, as well as Betty's, and to their exceeding joy they saw their fathers and mothers and all their relations and friends coming to meet them. And what a meeting it was and what a welcome they had!

Every vessel in the harbour hoisted its flag in honour of the children's return and the overcoming of that wicked old witch.

The boy, when Betty told how she had got her wings that enabled her to fly up the witch's stairs, was made much of by the people of Padstow Town and the friends of those seven little maids almost fought who should have him for their own.

How it was settled there is no need to tell, save only that he lived on Padstow quay and that he and Betty were always friends and loved each other dearly; and when they grew up they married and were as happy as the summer is long.

DUFFY AND THE DEVIL

AN OLD CHRISTMAS PLAY.

Open your doors, and let me in,
I hope your favours I shall win;
Whether I rise, or whether I fall,
I'll do my best to please you all.

A Christmas Play of St. George and the Dragon.

ASSOCIATED with Trove and the ancient family who lived, for many generations, in that pleasant place, there is a tradition that one old Squire Lovell wedded a poor girl solely because he believed her to be the best spinster and knitter in Buryan; but that all the fine stockings and other knitted garments with which she provided her husband were made by a devil. This droll formed the subject of an old Christmas Play which is all but forgotten.

The version given here is told in the form of a story, as the original play is long lost. One curious thing is that, near the beginning, the character Joan tells the heroine, Duffy, a story. This story is quite lengthy and it seems unlikely that there would have been time for it if told in a play. However, it is given as the next item in this book and where it should appear in this story you are given the option of reading it. You should also note that there is no mention of either St. George or the Dragon.

The Cast of Characters:-
Squire Lovell, of Trove.
Duffy, a poor girl, who became Madame Lovell.
Huey Lenine, Duffy's lover
Jenny Chygwin, Duffy's step-mother,

A Bucca-Boo, or Devil.

Betty, the witch of Trove Mill.

Joan, Squire Lovell's housekeeper.

Several ladies and gentlemen, and witches.

It began in Buryan Churchtown, in the cider-making time. Squire Lovell rode there on horseback to get help to gather in his apples and he came to the door of Jenny Chygwin. From inside the house he could hear two women, one old and one young, arguing within.

'Hullo! in there! Jenny, what's all the noise with you and the maid, I'd like to know?' he shouted.

Duffy rushed out, followed by old Jenny, her stepmother, who was beating the girl with the cord of her gown, saying, ' I will break every bone in her body. The lazy hussy is all the time out flirting and courting, with the boys. She will neither boil the porridge, knit nor spin.'

Duffy ran to the Squire, saying, 'Don't believe her, your honour. I do all the work, whilst she is drunk from morning till night, and my spinning and knitting is the best in Churchtown. Your stockings are nothing so fine as I can make.'

'Stop beating the maid, Jenny,' said the Squire, 'and choking me with dust from the skirt of your old swing-tail gown. And, Duffy, as you can spin and knit so well, come down to Trove and help my old house-keeper Joan, who is blind on one eye and can't see much with the other, as anyone can see by looking at the bad darns in my stockings and patches on my breeches. Come, use the stepping stone and jump up. You can ride down behind me.'

Without a pause Duffy jumped up behind the Squire and they rode off.

As they went Jenny muttered to herself: 'Aye, go with the old devil, and good riddance to bad rubbish.'

*****

It did not take long for the Squire and Duffy to reach his house in Trove. Pulling up outside the door the Squire called out to his housekeeper, 'Joan, come here and take in Duffy Chygwin, who has come down to help you knit and spin, give her some bread and cheese, and beer. Do you hear?' Having shouted his orders the Squire rode off, as he still needed to round up help for the apple gathering.

Joan came out and said, 'Oh, Duffy, my dear, I am glad to see you here, for I've badly needed help ever since that villain, Tom Chynance, put out the sight of one of my eyes because I saw his thievish tricks in stealing from the standings one night in Penzance.'

Joan then told Duffy a long story about how she lost her eye, which is omitted here (but if you like, you can read it now as it follows this story). She concluded by saying, 'Now you needn't eat any bread and cheese, as dinner will be ready soon. You can go up to the loft whenever you please and card wool to spin in the afternoon.'

*****

Duffy climbed to the loft, a room in which were fleeces of wool, a spinning-wheel and other appliances for spinning. Duffy sat herself down and started carding and making rolls of wool, which were placed in a winnowing sieve. After a while she got to her feet and exclaimed, 'Cuss the carding and spinning! What the devil shall I do now the wool is carded, for I can neither spin nor knit, and the devil take such work for me.'

Even as she said the words, from behind some wool came a devil, in the shape of a man, with half-cocked, squinting eyes and the barbed or forked tip of his tail just seen below his coat tails.

'My dear, here I am, come at your call, ready to do all you wish for very little pay,' he said. 'Only agree to go with me at the end of three long years, and for all that time I'll do your spinning and knitting and everything else you wish for, and even then, if you can tell me my name at three times of asking, you may go or stay, till another time.'

'Well, I don't mind much: anything for a change,' said Duffy, 'What did you say you were called? '

The Devil winked at her but did not fall into her trap. 'You have only to prick your arm and draw blood to sign our agreement you know,' he said.

'My word is as good as my mark, said Duffy. 'Spin and knit for me if you will and while you're doing it I'll go for a dance at the mill. Bolt the door behind me, so that no one may see who is doing the work.'

'Stop and let me take the measure of your foot,' said the devil, while stringing the spinning wheel as handy as if he had been used to spinning all his life.

Duffy wasn't at all scared at the Bucca-boo's appearance, because in old times people were so much used to dealings with the devil - women especially - that they didn't mind him. She went out by the outer door and stair, to merrily pass the day; and old Joan, hearing a rumble all through the house, thought her to be busy at work.

Duffy passed a great part of her time at Trove Mill, where a crowd of women met to take their turn at grinding, serging, and so on. Whilst some worked others told stories, sang, or danced on the green, near which grew many old oaks, sycamores, and elms, in a place still called the rookery.

There was a great friendship between Duffy and Old Betty, who worked the mill, because this old dame, having long had strange dealings, saw at once, by a stocking Duffy pretended to be knitting, that a stitch was always dropped and that the work was not hers.

In the evening, when she came in, Duffy heard the devil still spinning. She thought she would see him at work and try to learn something. Looking through the latch-hole she saw what she took to be a woman, seated, and spinning with a small treadle-turn such as is used for spinning thread and the wool-turn (with a wheel as large as that of a coach) put aside.

When she looked around she knew that it was only the devil dressed in clothes like those she wore. He had on a loose bed-gown, petticoat, and a large coarse apron with a large 'kerchief thrown loosely over his head and shoulders. As Duffy entered, he turned around and said, ' How are you, my dear? Here I am, you see, busy at work for you. See what I've already spun,' he continued, pointing to a heap of balls in the corner and skeins of yarn hanging on the walls.

She stood wondering, with eyes and mouth wide open, to see how easily the devil spun. Yet he seemed to do nothing with his hands but pull off the yarn whilst his foot worked the treadle, and a ball dancing on the floor wound itself up!

'Well,' said Duffy, 'I should have taken you for a woman if I hadn't chanced to spy your cloven foot, and your tail hanging down, and I don't much admire you in petticoats.'

'There's good reason for wearing them, however,' he replied. 'Besides, they are handy for such work, and if you will come here on Saturday night you will find, under that black fleece, ever so many pairs of stockings, both for you and the squire. I know his measure, and you'll see that they are a good fit for both of you. So now good night.'

Before she could wish him the same he disappeared, and all the yarn of his spinning along with him, leaving nothing to show that he had ever been there but a strong smell of brimstone.

Duffy didn't wait till dark night on Saturday, but went up to the wool-chamber about sunset. The Bucca-boo had just left work, and, having thrown off his petticoats, stood before her dressed like a sporting gentleman. He bowed as she entered and, handing her half-a-dozen pairs of stockings, all as strong as broadcloth and as fine as silk, said, 'Excuse me, my dear, from staying a moment longer, as I must be away before the Buryan bells are rung or some mishap may befall me.'

'I wish you well till I see you again, and thank you, Mr. What- shall-I-call-you?,' said Duffy, taking the stockings from his hand.

'You may call me captain,' he replied, and vanished in a flash of lightning with a roar of thunder that shook the house.

On Sunday morning, when Squire Lovell was getting ready to put on his velvet suit, that he might ride to church in grand state, as was his custom, Duffy brought him a pair of stockings suitable for the occasion.

'You see, master,' she said, 'that I haven't been idle. I've spun and knitted you a pair of lovely long stockings in three days and the work is very fine too.' He put on the stockings and admired the beautiful knitting and good fit. Then to show his delight at having such nice hose, the like of which were never on his legs before, he kissed Duffy again and again.

It was late when he reached Churchtown. After churching, he stopped, as usual, to exchange greetings with other gentry of Buryan. Everyone admired his fine stockings. The ladies enquired how and where he procured them, saying there was no one in the parish who could do such good work; one and all declared they were fit for a king.

The fame of Squire Lovell's stockings drew crowds of people to Buryan church on the following Sunday. Old and young wanted to feel his legs. They couldn't be satisfied with looking, and so they continued to come from farther and farther, Sunday after Sunday.

A few weeks later Joan, rather the worse for drink, was in the Squire's kitchen on a chimney-stool or bench in a broad and deep fire-place, such as used to be found in every West-country mansion, when wood and turf were the only fuel. She uttered awful groans and screeches until Duffy came to investigate. Then Joan said, 'Oh Duffy, you can't think what cramps I have in my stomach and wind in my head, that's making it quite light. Help me upstairs to bed, and you wait up to give the master his supper.'

The old housekeeper was helped to her bed by Duffy, who soon returned to seat herself on the chimney-stool.

As she was sitting there the door opened and Huey Lenine came in.

'What cheer, Duffy, my dear? Now you cannot say that the lanes are longer than the love, when I'm come to see you in this rainy weather,' he said.

'Joy of my heart,' said she, 'come by the fire and dry yourself.'

Huey sat on the outer end of the chimney-stool. After a long silence, Duffy eventually spoke, 'Why don't you speak to me then, Huey? '

'What shall I say then?' he replied.

'Say you love me, to be sure.'

'So I do.'

'That's a dear. That's a pretty waistcoat on you, Huey.'

'Cost pretty money too.'

'What did it cost then?'

'Two and twenty pence, buttons and all.'

'Take care of it then.'

'So I will.'

'That's a dear.'

There was another prolonged silence.

Finally, Huey continued, 'I'm thinking we will get married next year if you want.'

'Why don't you sit a little nearer then?'

'Near enough I believe.'

'Nearer the fire, I mean. Well, I'll be married to you any day, though you are no beauty, to be sure.'

Huey moved a little nearer.

Duffy, putting her hand on his face, said, 'Your face is as rough as Morvah Downs, that was ploughed and never harrowed they say; but I'll have you for all that and fill up with putty all the pock-mark pits and seams; then paint them over and make you as pretty as a new wheelbarrow.'

Suddenly they heard the squire outside calling his dogs. Duffy started up in a fright, seized some furze, and said, 'Master will be here in a minute, jump into the wood-corner and I'll cover you up with the furze.'

Huey hesitated. It did not look as if he would be able to hide there.

Seeing his hesitation, Duffy said, 'Then crawl into the oven: a little more baking will make you no worse.'

Huey climbed into the oven, opening on to the fire-place and behind the chimney-stool, just as the Squire entered and called out, 'Joan, take up the pie, if it's ready or raw. I'm as hungry as a hound.'

Duffy uncovered a pie that was baking on the hearth and said, 'Master, I have stayed up to give you your supper, because Joan has gone to bed very bad with a cramp in her stomach and wind in her head, so she said.'

'Why, I heard you talking when I came to the door, who was here then?' demanded the Squire.

'Only a great owl, master dear,' she replied, ' that fell down from the ivy-bush growing over the chimney and perched himself there on the stool, with his great goggle eyes, and stood staring at me and blinking like a fool. Then he cried Hoo! boo! Tu-wit, tu-woo; and, when you opened the door, he flew up the chimney the same way he came down.'

The Squire, satisfied with Duffy's explanation, advanced, and putting his foot on the hearth-stone, looked at his legs, saying, 'Duffy, my dear, these are the very best stockings I ever had in my life. I've been hunting all day, over moors and downs, through furze and thorns, among brambles and bogs, in the worst of weather, yet there isn't a scratch on my legs and they are as dry as if bound up in leather.'

The Devil, making himself invisible to the squire, rose behind Duffy and grimaced at the Squire.

Duffy spoke to the Squire, 'I may as well tell you, master, that I shan't knit much more for you, because Huey Lenine and I have been courting for a long time. We are thinking to get married before winter and then I shall have a man of my own to work for.'

'What! Huey Lenine!' shouted the Squire. 'I'll break every bone in his carcass if he shows his face near here. Why the devil would a young skit like you have it in your head to get married? Now, sit down a minute and I'll talk reason with you.'

The Squire sat down, close beside Duffy. The Devil tickled them both with his tail.

The Squire began, 'Give up your courting with Huey Lenine, And I'll dress you in fine silks and satins.'

Duffy replied,

'No, I'll never have an old man,
an old man like you.
Though you are Squire Lovell:
To my sweetheart I'll he constant and true,
though he works all day
with threshal and shovel.'

The Devil tickled the Squire behind the ears. The Squire moved nearer, placed his arm round her waist and said, 'You shall have a silk gown all embroidered in gold, jewels and rings, with such other fine things in an old oak chest, like you did never behold.'

Duffy replied,

'My sweetheart is young, lively and strong
with cheeks like a red rose;
But your time will not be long;
you have very few teeth and a blue-topped nose.
So keep your silks and keep your gold,
I'll never have a man so feeble and old.'

At this the Devil tickled them both. The Squire hugged and kissed Duffy, who made less and less resistance. Then he said, 'You shan't find me feeble, though I'm near sixty; I'm stronger still than many a man of twenty.'

'Your only son is now far away. If he came home and found you wed. What think you he would say?' argued Duffy.

'I hope he is already dead,' the Squire replied, 'or be killed in the wars some day. If he's alive he shan't enter my door, I'll give you my land, with all my store. You shall ride to church behind me upon a new pavillion, smarter than Dame Pendar or Madam Trezillian.'

Dear master, hold your flattering tongue,
nor think to deceive one so simple and young;
For I'm a poor maid, lowly born and bred -
one so humble you could never wed.
Keep your distance and none of your hugging;
You shall kiss me no more till you take me to church.
I'll never cry at Christmas for April fooling
like a poor maid left in the lurch.
Look! the sand is all down and the pie burned black.
With the crust too hard for your colt's-teeth to crack:
So off to the hall and take your supper.'

Duffy got up and took up from the hearth a pie, which had been baking there, and went out with it, followed by the Squire and Devil dancing. Huey crawled from the oven, saying 'Lack-a-day who can tell, now, what to make of a she-thing?'

By the time he has straightened up Duffy returned, and, assisted by the devil pushed him to the door, saying, 'Now, take yourself outside the door. Don't show your black face here anymore. Don't think I would wed a poor peasant like you when I may have a Squire of high degree.'

Duffy and the Devil danced till the Squire came back, whereupon the Devil vanished and the Squire took his place as Duffy's dancing partner.

*****

Later at Trove Mill, a long gossip took place over the new 'nine days' wonder' of Squire Lovell having wedded Duffy for the sake of her knitting. Some said she will behave like most beggars put on horseback, and all the women agreed that they would rather be a young man's slave, and work their fingers to stumps, than be doomed to pass a weary time beside such an old withered stock.

*****

Elsewhere Duffy (now Madame Lovell) is beheld walking up and down her garden, or in the hall, decked out in a gown with a long train, hanging ruffles at her elbows, ruff of monstrous size round her neck, towering head-dress, high-heeled shoes, with bright buckles, earrings, necklace, fan, and all other accessories of old-fashioned finery. The Bucca-boo is seen grinning, half-hidden, in the corner. Whilst Madam walked she sang,

> *'Now I have servants to come at my call,*
> *as I walk in grand state through my hall*
> *decked in silks and satins so fine.*
> *But I grieve through the day*
> *and fret the long night away*
> *thinking of my true-love, young Huey Lenine.*
> *I weep through many a weary long hour,*
> *as I sit all alone in my bower,*
> *where I do nothing but pine*
> *in dreaming of my true-love, young Huey Lenine.*
> *Would the devil but come at my call*
> *and take the old Squire - silks, satins, and all*
> *my jewels and rings so fine. Then, merry and gay,*
> *I'd work through the day*
> *and cheerily pass the nights away*
> *kissing my true-love, young Huey Lenine.'*

*****

Duffy often complained to Betty, the kind old witch, that she was very dissatisfied with her aged spouse. The old crone advised her to have patience and feather her nest, that she might secure a youthful successor to Squire Lovell, who wasn't likely to trouble her long. Notwithstanding her problems, she kept the Bucca-boo to his work, so that all her chests and presses were filled with stockings, blankets, yarn and home-spun cloth; and her husband was clad, from top to toe, in devil-made garments. Squire Lovell, as was his custom, was away hunting every week-day, from dawn till dark. The housekeeper and other servants, hearing a constant rumbling throughout the house like the noise of a spinning-wheel, only varied by the clicking of cards, thought their mistress was busy at work, when in fact she spent great part of her time at the mill.

The stocking that Duffy made out to be knitting, but never finished, had always a stitch down. By that old Betty suspected her of having strange dealings as well as herself.

Though the time seemed long and wearisome to Duffy, the term for which the devil engaged to serve her drew near its end: yet she was ignorant as ever of his true name, and gave herself but little concern on that account, thinking it might be just as well to go with a devil, who was so very obliging, as to remain with old Squire Lovell; for all the time this Bucca-boo became, as it were, her slave, he was well-behaved and never gave her the least reason to complain of his conduct.

Yet when she walked through Trove orchards, and saw the apple-trees weighed down with ripe fruit, she had some misgivings, in case her next abode might be less pleasant than Trove, besides, she thought that the devil, like most men, might be very civil in courtship but behave himself quite otherwise when he had her in his power.

Duffy, being much perplexed, made her troubles known to Betty, the witch, who, cunning woman as she was, hadn't found out the particulars of the bargain. She wasn't much surprised, however, when Duffy told her, because she knew that women and devils were capable of doing extraordinary things. Betty was somewhat troubled, but not much; for in old times, white-witches could perform almost incredible feats, by having devils and other spirits under their command. So, after twirling her thumbs a minute, and thinking what to do she said, 'Duffy, my dear, cheer up! I wouldn't like for you to be taken away before me. Now do what I tell you, and we'll find you a way to fool this young devil yet. So, tomorrow evening, soon after sunset, bring me down a black jack of your oldest and strongest beer. But before that, be sure you get the Squire to go hare-hunting. Fool him with an old story or anything else to make him go. Wait up till he comes back and note well what he may say. Go home now. Ask me no questions but do what I have told you!'

Next morning, the Squire noticed that his wife ate no breakfast, and, at dinner, observing that she seemed very sour and sad, and appeared not to want anything on the table, he said, 'My dear wife, how is it that you have been so melancholy of late? What is the matter with you? Don't I do as much to comfort you as any man can? If there's anything to be had, for love or money, you shall have it. You don't appear to have much appetite, honey; what would you like to eat?'

'I could just pick the head of a hare, if I had it,' she replied. 'I am longing for hare-pie but you have been so busy with the harvest that we haven't had one for weeks, and I'm feeling so queer that I must have one or the consequences will be awful to my unborn baby, and to you as well.'

'You know dear,' said the Squire, 'that the harvest is late. We have still much corn to get into the barn. Besides, it's also time that all should be ready for cider-making. I would do my best to catch a hare if that would please you,' he continued, after a bit; 'but don't you think that the old story about the child, that according to your fancy has been coming to and again for the last three years, is ever going to fool me to the neglect of corn and apples.'

'Hard-hearted, unbelieving wretch,' she replied, 'you don't deserve to be the father of my child. Know, to your shame, that innocent virgins, when first wedded are often deceived with false hopes. Now would you have our child disfigured for the sake of such little good as you are among the harvest people? An old man's baby,' she continued, 'is mostly a sad and wizened-looking object! Would you like to see ours with a face like a hare besides an ugly nose, and a mouth from ear to ear? Go, do, like a dear, and stop my craving; but in the evening, after some afternoon refreshment, will be time enough for you to start, that we may have one for dinner to-morrow.'

With coaxing, scolding, and hopes of paternal joys, she at length prevailed. As soon as the Squire and his dogs were out of sight, Duffy drew about a gallon of beer, that was many years old, into a strong leather jack, made small at the mouth like a jar, for convenience in carrying and took it down to the mill. Betty, after trying the liquor, said it would do, and told Duffy to go home, make the devil work till dark, wait up for her husband and keep her ears open to all he might say. When nearly dark and a few stars glimmered, Betty turned the water away from the mill-wheel and closed the sluices. Then, having put on her steeple-crowned hat and red cloak, she fastened the jack of beer to one end of a hempen girth, and her 'crowd', a violin-like instrument, to the other, slung them across her shoulder, under her cloak, took a black-thorn stick, closed her door, and away she went over the hill. She went up the glen between Trove and Boleigh, until she passed the Fuggo Hole, and there, amongst the thickets, she disappeared! All this area was well wooded and the upper part thickly covered with hazel, thorn, and elder; and a tangled undergrowth of briars, brambles, and furze, surrounded a wood called the Grambler Grove. Few persons liked to pass near this place, because strange noises were heard and fires often seen within it by night, when no one would venture near it.

Duffy waited up many hours after the servants had gone to bed, in great impatience for her husband's return. Her fears and doubts increased as she remained seated in the kitchen chimney-corner, attending to a pie on the hearth; that it might be kept hot for the Squire's supper. It came into her head at times, as a kind of forlorn hope, that the crafty old witch might somehow get the Devil to take her husband instead of herself. About midnight, however, her uneasy musings were interrupted by the dogs rushing in, followed by Squire Lovell, who seemed like one distracted, by the way he capered about and talked in broken sentences, of which his wife could make neither head nor tail. Sometimes he would caper round the kitchen, singing snatches of a strange dancing-time; then stop, try to recollect the rest and dance till tired out. At last the Squire sat down and told his wife to bring him a flagon of cider. After draining it, he became more tranquil, and, when Duffy asked if he had caught a hare, he answered, 'I've seen queer sights to-night, and the damned hare - as fine a one as ever was chased - was almost in the dogs' mouths all the while. We hunted her for miles, yet they couldn't catch her at all.' Then he burst out singing,

'To-morrow, my fair lady,
You shall ride along with me,
Over land and over sea,
Through the air and far away!,
'To strange countries you shall go,
For never here can you know.'

'I've forgotten the rest,' he said, after a pause, 'but give me supper and fill the tankard again. Then I will begin at the beginning, and tell you all about the strange things I've seen to-night. I wish you had been there; it would have made you laugh, though I haven't seen you so much as smile for a long time. But give me supper, I tell you again, and don't stay gaping at me like a frightened fool! Then, and not before, I'll tell you all about our uncommon chase, and we will ride "Over land, and over sea, with the jolly devil, far away, far away!" '

Duffy placed a pie on the table and helped the Squire.

After supper he came more to himself, and said, 'We hunted all the way down, both sides of the Bottom, from Trove to Lamorna without seeing a hare. It was then dark, but for the starlight: we turned to come home, and, up by Bosava, out popped a hare, from a brake of ferns close beside the water. She (the hare) went up on the moors. We followed close after, through bogs, furze, and brambles, helter-skelter, amongst mire and water. For miles we chased her - the finest hare that ever was seen, almost in the dogs' mouths all the way, yet they couldn't catch her at all. By the starlight we had her in sight all the way till far up the Bottom, between Trove and Boleigh: there we lost all sight and scent of her at last, but not till, tearing through brakes of brambles and thorns, we found ourselves in the Grambler Grove. And now,' he continued, after a drink from the flagon, 'I know for certain that what old folks say is true - how witches meet the Devil there of summer's nights. In winter they assemble in the Fuggo Hole, we all know; because one may then often hear the devil piping for their dance under our parlour floor - that's right over the inner end of the Fuggo. And now I believe what we took for a hare was a witch that we chased into this haunted wood. Looking through the thickets I spied, on a bare spot, surrounded by old withered oaks, a glimmering flame rising through clouds of smoke. The dogs skulked back and stood around me like things scared. Getting nearer, and looking through an opening, I saw scores of women - some old and ugly, others young and passable enough as far as looks go. Most of them were busy gathering withered ferns or dry sticks for the fire. I noted, too, that other witches, if one might judge by their dress, were constantly arriving - flying in over the trees, some mounted on ragworts, brooms, ladles, furze-pikes or anything they could get astride of. Others came on through the smoke as comfortable as you please, sitting on three-legged stools; and sat by the fire, with their black cats on their laps. Many came in through the thickets like hares, made a spring through the flame and came out of it as decent lasses as might see in Buryan Church of a holiday. A good large bonfire soon blazed up; then, by its light, I saw, a little way back sitting under a tree, who should you think? Why no less than old witch Betty, of the Mill. And by her side a strapping dark-faced fellow, that wasn't bad looking and that one wouldn't take to be a devil at all but for the company he was with, and the sight of his forked tail that just peeped out from under his coat-skirts. Every now and then Old Bet held to his mouth a black leather jack, much like ours, and the Devil seemed to like the drink by the way he smacked his lips. Now, said I to myself, I don't much dislike nor fear you, devil or no, as you are so honest as to drink hearty. So here's to you, wife!'

Duffy was very impatient, but took care not to interrupt the Squire. After draining the flagon, he continued to say,

'I should think the Devil got drunk at last by the way he capered when the witches, locked hand-in-hand, danced round the fire with him in their midst. They went round and round so fast one couldn't follow their movements as Betty beat up on her crowd the old tune of

"Here's to the Devil, with his wooden spade and shovel,

Digging tin by the bushel, with his tail cocked up." '

'After a while Old Bet stopped playing; the Devil went up to her, drained the jack, took from her the crowd, and sang a dancing-tune I never heard before. The words, if I remember right were,

"*I have knit and spun for her*

Three years to the day,

To-morrow she shall ride with me,

Over land and over sea,

Far away! Far away!

For she can never know

That my name is Tarraway!"

The witches then sung as a chorus,

"*By night and by day*

We will dance and play,

With our noble captain -

Tarraway! Tarraway!"

I thought the words odd for a dancing- tune, but devils and witches do queer things.'

'The witches, locked hand-in-hand, danced madder and faster, pulled each other right through the fire, and they weren't so much as singed, the bitches. They spun round and round so fast that at last, especially when the Devil joined in, my head got light. I wanted to dance with them and called out as I advanced, 'Hurrah! my merry Devil, and witches all!' In an instant, quick as lightning, the music stopped, out went the fire, a blast of wind swept away the embers and ashes, a cloud of dust and fire came in my eyes and nearly blinded me. When I again looked up they had all vanished. By good luck I found my way out of the wood and home. I'll have another hunt to-morrow and hope for better luck.'

The Squire drank another flagon of ale. Then, weighed down with fatigue and drink, he rolled from his seat on to the floor. Duffy covered him up. He often passed his nights like this when too drunk to go upstairs. As she threw a rug over him, and kicked a pile of rushes from the floor, in under his head, he murmured, 'To-morrow, we will ride over land and over sea, through the air and faraway! '

It was hours after sunrise when Squire Lovell awoke and found his wife sitting near him but she didn't say a word about his going hunting; in fact she indicated that she would rather not be left in the house alone or with only the servants. Late in the afternoon, however, he whistled to his dogs and away he went hunting again. As he had a mind to see, by daylight, the ground he'd covered, and where the witches danced, he took his way towards the Grambler Wood. Now Duffy hadn't been up-stairs for all that day, but, a little after sunset, she went up to the guest-chamber, as a large spare bedroom was called, to fetch something she much wanted. She took the garment from a hanging-press, and hastened to leave the chamber, but, when she passed round the bed she saw the Bucca-boo, standing before her, in the door-way. She never saw him looking so well, nor so sprucely dressed, before. From beneath a broad-brimmed hat and plume his coal-black hair fell in glossy curls on his shoulders. He wore a buff coat of fine leather, with skirts so long and full that they quite concealed his forked tail, or he might have coiled it round his waist for all we know. Anyhow there wasn't so much as the tip of it to be seen.

Duffy surveyed him, over and over again, from the golden spurs on his bright black riding-boots to the nodding plume on his high pointed hat, and thought she had never seen a more likely-looking fellow. Yet she was speechless from fear or surprise. The devil, advancing with stately step, doffed his hat, and bowing, said in courteous tones, 'Know, fair lady, the time is passed and some hours over that I engaged myself to work for you, and I hope that you have no reluctance to fulfill your part of our agreement.'

'Indeed no,' said she, 'I can't say I have much objection, as you are a very well-behaved, obliging devil and, during the three years that I have had the pleasure of your acquaintance, you have given me no reason to complain of your conduct. Yet,' she continued, after a moment's pause, 'I'd like to know where you live when at home and what sort of a country it is? I fear it may be rather hot, as you seem to be burnt very dark!'

'As to where my country is,' he replied, 'You wouldn't be much the wiser if I told you all about it, because up till now you have seen so little of the world that there would be great difficulty in making you understand. As a proof, however, that my country's climate isn't much to be complained of, you see me strong and healthy enough; besides, I'm not so dark-skinned under my clothes; and, if you were burned as black as myself, I would love you all the same.'

'I can't quite make up my mind,' said she, 'though no doubt you would please me as well, and make a better husband than Squire Lovell, who, if he isn't drunk, snores all night with his face to the wall. If I went how would you convey me to your far country?'

'I have brought to the Grambler Grove a noble steed,' he replied, 'that will go over land and sea, or fly through the air with lightning speed. Now do make haste, dear, and get you ready for my horse is very impatient to be left alone; he may whistle for me and shake down the chimney-tops, or paw the ground and make all the country tremble; yet he is as gentle as a lamb when mounted. So come along as you are; there's no time for delay,' said he, offering his hand.

'If you please,' said Duffy, shrinking back, ' I would like to stay in Trove a little longer.'

'Now, no nonsense,' said the devil, in an angry tone; 'You know that I have been true to my word, as every gentleman ought, and trust you will abide by our bargain: and as for your knowing my name,' added he, with a haughty air, 'that's impossible, because it is long since that I, like other persons of quality, have only been known by my title, and even that is not familiar to vulgar ears.' Assuming his ordinary courteous manner, he said, 'Yet, my love, for mere form's sake I'll ask you three times if you like! Besides, I'm curious to know what sort of a guess you will make at it. So now, for the first time asking, tell me if you can, what is my name? '

'My dear Mr. Devil,' said she, 'don't you take offence if I happen to misname you in my ignorance. Now aren't you my lord Beelzebub! '

'No! be damned,' he replied, choking with anger, 'how could you even think me such a mean, upstart devil as Beelzebub, whose name isn't known in the place where I belong; and, even here, among those best acquainted with him, nobody ever heard of his grandfather! Now I hear my horse shaking his bridle and, for the second time, I ask you my name? '

'Pray excuse my ignorance and don't you be vexed,' said she, 'for I don't doubt but you are a grand gentleman when at home and no other, I think, than Prince Lucifer!'

'What? Lucifer!' he exclaimed, more than ever enraged; 'you make me mad but to think that I should ever be taken for one of such a mean tribe as Lucifer, who is no better than the other. As for me, I wouldn't be seen in their company. None of their family were ever known or heard of in this country till lately. Great indeed is your want of sense,' he continued, with a scornful air, 'to take me for one of these upstarts. Yet, many fools - if one may judge by their fears - seem to reverence them; nay almost to worship them. But crafty folks, who profit by fools' fears, haven't a good word to say of these new buccas behind their backs, nor yet of their country; for that, they say, is full of burning brimstone, and one may well believe it, for when any of the tribe come here they stink of sulphur. But one like you - born and bred in Buryan Churchtown - can't have any notion of the antiquity and dignity of my family! If you hadn't been the loveliest of Buryan ladies I would never have condescended to spin for you. And now, for the third and last time, I ask what is my name?' On the same breath he added, 'Come! Give me your hand love, and let's away, for you can never guess it.'

Duffy didn't feel much reluctance to go with him, yet was proud to outwit the devil and answered, 'Don't you be in such a hurry, old gentleman, Buryan people may not be so ignorant as you think them; they live near enough to St. Levan witches to know something of devils and their dealings. You are Tarraway - you won't deny it! '

'No, by my tail,' said he, almost speechless with surprise; 'I am too proud of my ancient name to disown it. I'm fairly beaten; it's provoking though to be outwitted by a young thing like you and I can't think however you found it out. But true as I'm a gentleman, if you don't go with me now, the time will come when you'll wish you had, and one day you shall spin for me yet.'

Duffy shrunk back, and, in a moment, thick smoke gathered around Tarraway; the room became dark; and he disappeared amid a blaze of lightning and a rattling peal of thunder, that shook the house from end to end.

Duffy, much frightened, ran down stairs, and, as she entered the hall, in tore old Joan, terrified out of her wits by the kitchen chimney-top rattling down on the hearth where pots, kettles, and pans were all smashed. Their dread was much increased by finding throughout the house a smother of burning wool. Other women servants ran shrieking into the hall. Old Joan said she felt a fit coming on; but while she looked about for a place to fall down and have her fit in comfort; into their midst rushed the Squire, with nothing on but his hat, shirt, and shoes. At this sight all the women began to swoon. The Squire stood for some time, looking on, like one distraught, till the women came to. They all run out except his wife. She asked him how he came home in such a plight and where he had left his clothes. The Squire told her that when he came to the Grambler he had a fancy to see by daylight the place where Old Nick and his witches had their dance the preceding night. He entered and searched all round - over bare places, between the trees, and elsewhere, but saw no signs of any fire having been made in the wood; there wasn't even a handful of ashes, or the grass so much as burnt on the spot where he was sure he saw a bonfire blazing the night before.

He turned to leave this haunted place, by taking his course down the Bottom, but, when he was just out of the wood, a blinding flash of lightning surrounded him like a sheet of flame, whilst he was stunned by louder thunder than he ever heard before. When he recovered his senses and opened his eyes he found that all his home-spun woollen garments were burned from his back, leaving him as he then stood. He believed it was all done by witchcraft, because he saw their devilish doings. He told his wife to fetch him a coat, stockings, and breeches.

Duffy, frightened to go upstairs alone, called Joan to accompany her, and great was her terror to find that every article of Tarraway's work had disappeared from chests and presses - nothing was left in them but Squire Lovell's old moth-eaten garments covered with dust and ashes. He was very dissatisfied with his old clothes, but there was no help for it.

As clever a conjuror as any in the west country was fetched. He declared that it was all exactly as Squire Lovell thought - the devil and witches had served him out because he wanted to pry into their doings, and had chased one of them in the form of a hare. The wise man nailed old horse-shoes over the doors, and promised, for little pay in proportion to his services, that he would take Trove and the Squire's household under his protection, so that they need fear no more mischief from witchcraft, nor bad luck.

Duffy, by the witch's aid, had a happy riddance of Tarraway, yet greater troubles were in store for her. Squire Lovell, disliking to be seen again wearing his old stockings, would neither go to church nor to market, and instead of hunting from dawn till dark, he stayed indoors all day, in a very surly mood, to keep his wife at her spinning. But she knew no more how to spin than when she summoned the Bucca-boo to work for her.

The Squire having forbade Betty the witch to come near his house, Duffy had little chance to see her; but one Thursday evening when he was off guard - up to the blacksmith's shop in Boleigh, to hear the news from returning market-people, as was his custom - Duffy hastened off to Mill and made known her troubles, and the next market-day Betty went to Penzance and bought the best stockings she could get. On Sunday morning Duffy brought them to her husband and passed them off as her own work; but he wasn't at all satisfied, because they weren't so fine and soft as those he had been accustomed to for three years. He wouldn't go to church in them; he went hunting, however, and returned very cross, for his new stockings didn't protect his legs from brambles, furze and wet, like Tarraway's. He again stayed indoors to keep his wife to spin, and Duffy was obliged to twirl her wheel all day though she only spoiled the wool, for unless he heard the sound of the wheel turning or the cards, he would be up to the wool-chamber door calling out, 'Are you asleep Duffy, lazy slut that you are, I haven't heard cards nor turn for an hour or more, and unless you very soon make me better stockings than the rags on my legs, and good breeches too, I'll know the reason why, that I will, you lazy faggot you. What the devil else did I marry you for I'd like to know.' She would threaten to card his face if he entered, so they led a cat and dog life for months, that seemed years to Duffy, shut up as she was in a dusty wool-loft and not a soul to comfort her or to share her griefs. Her spirits sunk and her beauty faded fast, she thought it had been better by far to have gone with the devil, than lead such an irksome life with old Squire Lovell. Often she prayed Tarraway to come for her, but he turned a deaf ear to her cry and was never more seen in Trove.

By good luck, when winter and muddy roads came, the Squire took it into his head one Sunday morning to put on his leather boots and jog off to church, that he might learn what was going on in the rest of the world.

It was the Sunday before Christmas. He wished his wife to mount behind him, but she, pretending illness, begged to be excused and said she would be glad to accompany him next time.

Duffy watched her good man spurring his Dobbin till he was clear of Trove town-place, then down she ran to Mill. and told old Betty that unless she got a speedy release from her irksome task she would drown herself in the mill-pool.

Bet sat a moment, twirling her thumbs so quick that one could hardly see them spinning round each other, and said, 'No, my dear child, don't you think of such a thing yet, young and handsome as you are it would be a pity. Let's try a scheme that I've thought of. A woman never should despair of finding a trick to fool an old man, and if need be the old witch will stir her stumps and trot again to help you. If one plan don't serve we'll try another, for as the old saying is "nobody ever got out of a ditch by grunting," what's just popped into my head may answer!'

'Do tell me what it is,' said Duffy.

'No, there's no time now,' Betty replied. 'You have wasted so much already in moaning about your griefs instead of thinking how to get rid of them, like a sensible body ought, that old Squire will soon be back from church, and he mustn't know that you have been here, so only mind now what I am going to tell you.'

'Next Saturday, being Christmas-Day, the Squire will no doubt go to church and desire you to go with him; by all means go, and when, as usual after churching, you stop at the cross to exchange greetings with other gentry, I'll come near enough for you to hail me with "A Merry Christmas to you Betty, and a Happy New Year when it comes." I shall wish you the same, and you invite me, before the Squire, to come up in the evening to taste your Christmas beer. And in the afternoon when, according to custom, there will be a hurling match from Churchtown to Boleigh, the Squire and you, with scores of gentlefolks, on horseback and on foot, will be near the goal to see the ball brought fairly in, and to stop any fighting; then look out for me, give your kindest greetings again, and don't be surprised at anything you may hear and see, or if you are don't show it, and invite me again to partake of your Christmas cheer. That's all I have to tell you now,' she said, opening her door for Duffy to depart, but going a few steps out on to the Green she continued, 'It doesn't cost you any pain, no not a bit, to speak kindly to a poor body now any more than before you became Madam Lovell, and as good a lady as the best in Buryan, for you are no ways vain; but if you had ever shown any scornful pride be assured I would never have gone a trotting for you, nor do what I intend, to get you relieved of your troubles: besides it isn't your fault that you can neither knit nor spin, you never had a kind mammy to teach you. And no one can blame you for deceiving old Squire Lovell - lying and deceit come to us poor women by nature - so hasten home, leave the rest to me, and hope for better times.'

Duffy got home just in time to see that dinner was ready when her husband returned in a good temper after his morning's ride.

'Duffy, my dear,' said he, as she assisted him to pull off his boots, 'I wish you had gone to church, everybody was enquiring for you, and asking what was become of us this long time that they hadn't seen sight nor sign of us. And some of the women - cuss their itching curiosity they can never be satisfied - wanted to roll down my boot-tops and undo my knee-buckles that they might have a peep at my stockings. But on Christmas-Day come along with me, they won't be so forward if you are there.'

Duffy replied, 'My darling man, I'll go with all my heart and see if they carry their impudence so far again, and now dear, make a hearty dinner, and tell me all the news you have heard.'

Christmas-Day in the morning, Duffy, as richly attired as any lady in Buryan, mounted on a pillion behind her husband and away they went to church. After service, a great number assembled at the Cross and sung old carols. Squire and Madam Lovell exchanged many kindly compliments with the Cardews, Harveys, Noys, Fenders, Vivians, Gwennaps, and other ancient gentry of Buryan, who were waiting for their steeds.

Whilst wishing her neighbours a Merry Christmas Madam Lovell had kept a sharp look out for old Betty; but had nearly given up all hopes of seeing her and was about to mount behind the Squire, when glancing around for the last time she spied her steeple-crown and red mantle among the crowd of singers. Madam went to meet her, shook hands heartily and said, 'Good morrow to you Dame Chymellan, how are you? I am glad to see you looking so well and wish you a Merry Christmas and a Happy New Year, and many of them. I hope you liked the sermon and the singing, and so on;' - we can't tell all the fine compliments that passed so long ago.

'Thank your honour, and I wish you the same,' the old dame replied, making a low curtsey to Duffy. Then turning round to other gentlefolks, she continued to wish all their honours - as she styled them - the compliments of the tide, calling each by name as she curtsied to everyone.

Now there was nothing remarkable in Betty's civil words; but as she stood close beside the Squire, who was on horseback, and bestowed her old-fashioned greetings at every curtsey, an unseemly noise was heard from her vicinity. Squire Lovell got vexed, the ladies looked confused, glanced at him and rode off.

Betty, however, without appearing to hear or to heed anything, mounted her horse and jogged away with Dame Pendar; Squire Lovell and others going the same road. As they parted Duffy said to her, 'Betty be sure that you come up early to try our Christmas-cake and ale.'

'Thank your honours I will,' she replied, turning off to the Mill.

It was customary for the Squire's tenants, and all who choose, to assemble at his house every night from Christmas-Eve till twelfth-night, to freely partake of his abundant cheer and help in the merry disports of the tide; yet he wasn't at all pleased because his wife had invited the old dame. 'I shouldn't have minded her coming at any other time,' he said, 'but today a good many from the hurling will come home with us and pass the evening; I hope however, she will be on her best behaviour before the quality. To be sure one doesn't like to offend the spiteful old witch for fear of her tricks.'

In the afternoon Squire Lovell and his wife, with many others - mostly on horseback - were got together near Daunce-Mayn when old Betty stalked in to their midst and just such another scene was enacted there as took place in Churchtown. Many who came from a distance went down to Trove to pass a merry Christmas night.

A score or more of ladies and gentlemen, seated in the hall, pledged each other in hot-spiced-ale, brandy, punch and wine, when Betty, Joan and others entered, holding aloft their horns of foaming liquor. The Squire, fearing another display of Betty's unbecoming behaviour, rose in haste to prevent her drinking their healths with all the honours. 'Stay a moment Betty,' he said, 'come into the kitchen, I must tell you that twice already today you have made me ashamed of you, how could you do so and show so little respect for the company both in Churchtown and Boleigh? '

'O dear master, you mustn't mind such a trifle as that,' replied she, without budging an inch, 'for it will soon be all the same with Madam there, your honour's wife, if you keep her to spin so much, she won't be able to help it for her life. You may look scared and misbelieving, but indeed she won't; No! No more than I can whenever I move quick, or curtsey to your honours as I am, in duty, bound to do; and if your honours would like to hear how it happened to me I'll tell you.'

Many of the company having intimated that they would like to hear how she became in such a condition. Squire Lovell placed her in a settle near the hearth, she emptied her horn and began her tale:-

'Know then, your honours, that in my first husband's time, - more than thirty years ago, - we lived at Trevider. I did outdoor work and helped old mistress besides, when there was extra house work, such as great brewings, cheese-making, the baking and roasting at feasten-tides, spinning for the weavers, besides the regular spinning of winter's nights, and such like. Although I say it, there wasn't a brisker lass in Buryan than I was then; just like mistress there, your honour's wife. There was no woman and but few men that could beat me in shaking threshed wheaten sheaves, leading trusses, branding turves, raking roots and grass, reaping, aye, or binding either on a push; and I could mow as well as any man. Old master used to say that at the winnowing-sheet, there wasn't my equal in the parish for handling the sieve and kayer (coarse sieve), and that I made a better sample of corn, and not half so much after-winding and waste, as any other windster he ever met with; but I needn't blow my trumpet any more on that score. My old mistress, Madam Pendar, was a noted spinster, as you may have heard, and of winter's nights she, with her servant maidens and I, took our places at the spinning wheels; master and the servant men carded and sung, three-men's songs or told old drolls the while. My spinning-work was soon equal to Madam Pendar's although she would never allow it; but my yarn was strong, even, and fine, just like your honour's wife's,' said Betty, addressing Squire Lovell to fasten his attention.

'And often I was kept spinning all day for days running, just like mistress there. But one Christmas night everybody belonging to Trevider, young and old, went off in a Guise-dance, except old mistress and I. 'Now they are all gone, Betty,' said she, 'and left us all alone, see if we don't enjoy ourselves." Mistress drew a good jug of strong old ale, boiled, sweetened, and spiced it whilst I roasted the apples; we brewed a drink fit for a king; for hours we pledged each other's good health and drank to our heart's content. Over a while mistress began to brag of her spinning, she was proud of her work and so was I of mine, just like your honour's wife. I shall ever remember that Christmas-night and how cheery the old hall looked with the Christmas-log burning bright, and faggots of oak and ash blazing up the chimney, showed every window, dresser and wall decked in holly, box, and ivy; with branches of bays and rosemary around the pewter flagons, plates, and platters, that shone like silver among the Christmas greenery.

Old mistress boasted much of her spinning, and wager'd a bottle of brandy - which she placed on the board - that she would spin a pound of wool in a shorter time, and make a finer yarn than I could. I took her to her word, rolled up the rushes from the floor, to make a clear run all the length of the hall, and placed our turns, while mistress weighed and carded the wool, divided the rulls, and gave me my choice of them.

When all was ready, to cheer our hearts and put life in our heels, we each drank a noggin of brandy. Then I tripped backward and forward as light as a feather, and for more than three hours we twirled our wheels by the bright fire-light, keeping good time together. My yarn was even and fine as a flaxen thread; just like that spun by my lady there, your honour's wife, and I was then about her age. I had nearly spun my pound of wool, and never felt in better heart for dancing to the turn, when, as bad luck would have it, my twadling-string - weakened with so much stepping backwards - burst. I fell to the ground, and ever since I've been in the sad predicament that so surprised your honours. Though it's comforting to have companions in affliction,' said she, after a pull at the flagon, 'yet from the regard I have for your honour and mistress there, I have spoke of my ailment to warn you that as sure as I sit here with a broken twadling-string it will soon be the same with my lady there, if it's true, what I do hear, that you keep her to spin from morn till night most every day of the year. When that do happen you will be frightened into fits; old mistress was so scared that she nearly lost her senses, she thought the house was falling about her ears, to save herself she snatched the bottle and tore up stairs; next day she was found asleep under a bed with the empty bottle close by her head.'

Old Betty's story rather surprised the company, and Squire Lovell, much concerned, said 'I'm glad you told me, Betty, now drink another horn full like a dear; I wouldn't for the world that my darling Duffy should be in such a plight, nevermore shall she spin from this very night. I would go bare legged all my life, rather than such a mishap should befall my wife.'

The entertainment concluded with a dance, to music made by Father Christmas.

The End

ONE-EYED JOAN'S TALE

'SIT down, Duffy, my dear; eat some bread and cheese; don't be afraid to drink the beer, it's all my own brewing,-the more you take the more good it will do you; and I will tell you how I lost the sight of my eye.

Now, I know for sure and certain that there isn't a ranker witch in all the country round than old Betty down in the cove and her great long lanky Tom isn't a bit better than the St. Levan witches; they have all got strange dealings, I can assure you.

The last Christmas Eve that ever was, I went to Penzance to buy a pair of shoes for myself, and some thread, buttons and things to mend the tears in master's clothes; for he, good man, do what I may, is always as ragged as a colt: but how shouldn't he be when he is out hunting all the time, from the break of day till dark night, through bogs and brambles, furze and thorns, in all sorts of weather? No clothes could ever stand on his back, if one made them of leather. But he wouldn't care a cuss if he hadn't a coat to his back nor breeches to his legs, - no, not he, so give him his horse and his dogs and his old crony, squire Pender, to have a carouse with every night.

As I said, I made up my mind to jog off to town. As I dearly like company and Betty down in the cove is always ready for a jaunt, thinks I to myself if she is a witch she will never hurt me, as I never crossed her in my life; and, witch or no witch, bad company is better than none they say; so I put on my hat and cloak, took my basket and stock, then off to the cove. Down by the end of Bosava lane I met two of Tom's great skates of maidens, with cowls, seemingly full of fish, on their backs. We stopped and had a chat. They always carry something in the cowls under the ferns that they make more of than the fish; whenever they call at any house and they find the men out of the way, they give the tip-of-the-wink to their wives, for they all like a drop, and the jars of rum, gin, or brandy, are dragged out from among the ferns under the fish. If the wives haven't money they will give meat or other things of twice the value, and they never know when they had had enough of a good thing, as I tell master and squire Pender, when they are both so drunk that they can neither see, stand, nor lie on the ground without holding on, that they destroy good liquor, instead of taking a little like I do, in moderation. Tom's girls asked me to take a dram. I told them I thought a thimbleful or so would do me good, as I had a long walk before me, and to come up to the squire's sometime in the Christmas holidays and I would remember their kindness. It wasn't much after noon when I got to the cove, but there wasn't a soul to be seen about the place. All Tom's children, that belong home, were, according to custom, down by the seaside, ranging over the rocks, gathering limpets or paddling about in the sea-winter or summer no difference, a hardier set were never reared; and, to see the piles of limpet-shells about outside of the house, one would think they ate nothing else but limpets and periwinkles.

The door of Tom's house was shut. I heard him inside saying something to Betty. I listened, but couldn't make out what they were talking about. That I might know what was going on, before lifting the latch, I took a peep through the latch hole and saw Tom sitting down on the chimney-stool, with Betty standing alongside, taking some ointment from a box which she held in her hand and rubbing it over Tom's eyes, mumbling all the time something that sounded like the verse of a charm. There seemed to be other voices within as well. I listened with all my ears to find out was going on. Many said that Betty was something worse than a white witch and Tom's piercing dark eyes made some believe that he had all the power of the evil eye; yet they are beautiful eyes too. You have seen the bright sky shining in a smooth pool, when the water seemed as deep as the sky was high; such are the dark-hazel eyes of Chenance, until an angry cloud passes over them; then the lightning-flashes dart on those who dare cross the man and make cowards quail.

Not being able to hear from the door, I went round to a little window (a sort of air-hole always open), in the chimney-end, looking out over the brook. When there I was not much the wiser, because there is such a brake of ivy and honeysuckle growing all over the walls, the roof and wreathing together round the chimney-stack, that there is scarcely a stone or any thatch to be seen, and a thicket of sweet-briar sprouting out under the window hid all within from sight; and, with the murmuring of the waters, the singing and tweeting of the robin-red-breasts that flew in and out of their nests on the rafters, and the buzzing of the bees that had long made their home in the hollow wall, flying about the same as on a summer's day, hindered me from hearing what was going on within. The windows of Tom's house looked towards the sea. The door is on the land side; so I returned to the door side and sat down a moment on the bench placed under the ash-trees that are planted round the house according to the old custom for the sake of keeping the adders away. Then, going to the door and peeping through the finger-hole again, I saw that Tom rose to come out and noted that Betty put the box of ointment in a hole beside the chimney. When Tom came close to the door I lifted the latch and entered. After all the "how-de-does," "how glad I am to see Joan," and so on, out went Tom.

As soon as he was gone out of hearing, says Betty, "Now we will have a good drop to ourselves as it is Christmas-eve; it will do us good. I shan't be able to go to town," she said, "because I have been very bad all day with the wind in my stomach and can't get well all I can do, for all that I have been standing on my head, taking milk and soot, brandy and rue, gin and pepper and everything else I ever heard to be good for curing the mullygrubs."

"I'll take a thimbleful, just to drink your health and a merry Christmas to you, with all my heart," I said. She asked me if I would take a cup of sweet drink, or a glass of rum or brandy, or some of both. Betty is noted for making the best of sweet drink, but as that is rather cold I told her to put a dash of rum in the sweet drink and I would take a drop of brandy after. Then she went to the larder that is screened off in the other end, and all shelved round with old wreck timber, to get the liquor. As I said before, everybody had often wondered how the great long Tom's eyes were always so bright and piercing, but now I knew that it must be all owing to the fairy ointment or witch-salve that they made and used. "Well," thought I, "if the salve is so good for his eyes it will do no harm to mine, as they are rather dull sometimes." So, as soon as Betty entered the larder, I took the box of green ointment from the hole where she had covered it up with some ferns, and, taking the least bit on the top of my finger, put it to my right eye. The confounded stuff had no sooner touched my poor eye than I felt as if a stick of fire, or all the needles and pins in my pocket, had been thrust into it!

Betty remained, by good luck, a long time in the larder, sucking a drop from the jar by herself, I suppose. Before she came out I had fixed myself in the dark corner of the chimney and dragged the brim of my hat down over the right side of my face (I wore my best steeple-crowned, broad-leaved beaver) and never made sight nor sign to her of anything. After we had drunk each other's healths three or four times, in some capital French brandy, the pain went off a little, but I couldn't think where in the world she could contrive to stow away all the children by night: they have ten or a dozen home, besides ever so many away to sea. Tom don't know himself how many she's got, half the time, for Betty never makes any fuss about bringing them into the world. No one comes near her (that anybody knows of), but all are born by the hearth,- the last child is turned out of the straw and bramble basket, where it lays on green ferns and the new one, wrapped in a few clean rags, is put on some fresh ferns in its place. Then she goes about her work. There is no fuss about the matter. Ten to one if Tom knows anything about it for days after. I asked Betty where all of them contrived to roost.

"Wherever they have a mind to," she said; "some of the smallest (except the babies) get up and stretch themselves in the bed, round the bed and under the bed, as they like; and look there at that little bunk, in the top of the wood-corner, that Tom made out of some wreck timber the other day, that the bigger boys might have a place to themselves. As you see, he put in two strong beams to reach across from the wall to the side of the chimney, then put some planks upon them. To be sure the place isn't so deep in as it ought to be for the boys to stretch out at full length, as the outside only just reaches to the bowings of their knees; but what matter? they like the place well enough and their legs hanging down over, when they have a mind to stretch out, will make them grow all the longer! Half the time they are never in the house at all by night, but sleep down in the boat, when she is moored to the ring-rock and all afloat."

"Well," I said, "there isn't a healthier nor a handsomer set of boys and maidens in the parish than yours," and, to give the devils their due, no more there isn't.

"Come, you shall take another dram, Joan" she said, "to drink health and long life to them all, in some of as good French brandy as ever you tasted. All our maidens, as well as our boys, swim like gulls and dive like shags. They will no more be drowned than a conger. What do you think of the freak of the maid Jenefer? After hearing a lot of stories about the mermaids combing their hair and singing on the half-tide rocks, she took it into her head to play the same pranks, in the summer evenings, on the rock you know we call the mermaid's rock. There she would fix herself to sing with the tide rising over her and there remain until she was more swimming than sitting, when she would dive under the waves and swim ever so far away before come ashore. Now, ever so many of the rest carry on the same fun, so that sailors going by, who hear their songs and see them seated on the rocks, would swear that they saw a whole shoal of mermaids in the cove."

When we had drunk to the health of the mermaids, I ventured to wipe the water from my face with my apron and to open my anointed eye, and oh! the Lord deliver me from what I saw - the place was full of sprites and spriggans; in all the folds of the nets and sails, that were thrown over the key-beams, in the clews of ropes that hung from the rafters, troops of small-people were cutting all sorts of capers; some of them were playing in pairs at see-saw all along the railing; the little creatures were tossing up their heels, waving their feathered caps and fans as they launched up and down on the merest bits of stick or green twigs; numbers of them were swinging in the cobwebs that hang from the rafters, or riding the mice in and out through the holes in the thatch.

I noted that all the little men were dressed in green pinked out with red, and had feathered caps on their head, high riding-boots with silver spurs on their heels; their ladies, if you please, were all decked out in the grand old fashion - their gowns were of green velvet with long trains, some looped up with silver chains and bells or tassels; other had their trains sweeping behind them as they walked in grand state, on their way up and down and all about the place: they seemed to think there was nobody in the house but themselves forsooth, prancing about in their high-heeled shoes, sparkling with diamond buckles. The little women all wore high-crowned, steeple-hats like mine, to make themselves look taller I suppose, the vain little mortals, with wreaths of the most beautiful flowers of all colours around them, sprigs and garlands on all the other parts of their dress and in their hands as well, flirting their fans in the faces of the men. They were the sauciest little mortals I ever did see. What puzzled me the most was to see so much sweet flowers with them at that time of the year.

Though old mistress, the squire's mother, the Lord rest her, had often told me that the fishermen, when out to sea on moonlight nights, see the small-people's gardens down among the carns, blooming with the gayest flowers all the year round, and the most soothing music is often heard by them resounding along the shore, from sawn to carn, I wasn't much frightened to see them, for I had heard about them and their doings ever since I was born, and knew then that Betty had the secret (among many others she had learned in her strange dealings) of making the fairy ointment, that made me see with my anointed eye all that was going on in the fairy world. When I peeped round into the wood-corner, under the boys' bunk, I spied some of the ugly spriggans seated in the dark corner looking very gloomy, because they are doomed to guard the treasures, and to do many other irksome things that the merry small-people are free from; besides, the small-people are very restless and changing, even when they hold their fairs: for these merry meetings, to show their vanities, only last an hour or two.

Whilst looking into the dark corner, I heard the strains of sweet but unearthly music outside the house and, looking again around the house, all was changing. Ever so many robin red-breasts were coming in through the open window and, perching themselves on the key-beams, sang as if they had a mind to split their throats. The tittering wrens left the mossy balls of nests they had built themselves under the eaves, and, hopping and flying, came down on the clews of ropes, to do all they were able with their tweeting to increase the music that was now close at hand under the little window, through which a moment later, a troop of the small-people entered, playing such sweet strains on the pipes, flutes, flageolets and other instruments they had made with green reeds of the brook and shells of the shore, as made even the pert robins keep silence after they had tried in vain to equal the notes of the fairy strains.

The fairy-band stepped down most gracefully from the little window-seat, on to the floor, and were closely followed by pairs of the little ladies and some few of their gentlemen, all bearing bunches of herbs or flowers. All walked in orderly procession, bowed or curtseyed to dame Chenance, and stood at a little distance behind her until some elderly fairy gentlemen, who closed the procession, came up and cast their herbs into her apron. I saw among them many bunches of the four-leaved clover (with which the ointment is made that enabled me to see all their doings). They brought her sprigs of agrimony, bettony, camomile, vervain, mouse-ear and hundreds of other plants from down and moor that I don't know the names of. With these she makes her salves and charmed lotions. Now, all the fairies who had been enjoying themselves in all parts of the house, came around the musicians and the others who had returned with herbs and flowers. Betty seemed to be so used to what was going on that she did not look surprised, and I said nothing to let her know what I saw. She is always as clean as water can make her, or as the whitest shell on the shore; that day she had on, as usual, her dark russet-coloured quilted petticoat, with a white jacket of her own knitting made of the softest lamb's-wool yarn. For the sake of showing her dark chestnut curling hair, she seldom puts a hat and never a cap, on her head; whether good or bad, she is always clean and handsome. As soon as the small people who bore herbs retired, others approached, and poured over her dress (from the unopened flowers or bottles of the foxglove) such dews or dyes as they gathered from sea or land, or God knows whence. The dyes had no sooner touched her dress than it was changed into a three-piled velvet of the same colour; the jacket became the finest and softest cloth, of a rich cream colour. Then others laid silver cord all over the quiltings that divided out the petticoat into diamond-shaped squares. The whole troop then advanced to deck out the dame with their flowers. Many brought little nosegays of the sky-coloured speedwell, with its flowers so like innocent eyes; other of the pimpernel, its dainty blossoms and globes of seed; the forget-me-not, eyebright, sweet lady's tresses, violets, heath-bells and abundance of the dainty little bells-blue, pink, or white-that we find in such plenty on the moors in summer time, and hundreds of other fairy flowers like stars, bells, or butterflies that I never heard any names for. All these flowers were made up into the daintiest little sprigs of nosegays you ever saw-all of the same size yet all differently composed. These delicate sprigs were stitched all over the silver-corded petticoat; a sprig in the middle of each square. Some very tiny flowerets were placed in a ground of delicate branching moss and flowers of wild grass; others they placed on the smallest leaves of the lady fern, or of the camomile plant. Near the bottom of her skirt, all around, the little ladies made a wreath of small bramble leaves, intermixed with the most delicate bramble roses and their berries red and black. There was little other ornament on the jacket than the finest of lace turned over collar and cuffs and a few such sparkling jewels to fasten it as dazzled my eyes-even the charmed one.

Many of the little creatures perched themselves on the top of the high-backed chair, on which dame Chenance sat and even on her shoulders that they might come to arrange every curl and every hair on her head. Some took the lids off the pretty little urns they bore in their hands and poured a perfume on her head, that spread the sweetest odour around the place. I very much admired the neat little urns, and their grooved lids, but when I picked up one it was only the seed-cup of the wild poppy. And her apron! oh, I forgot to tell how her check apron became (after she had placed the herbs away) a cross-barred shiny silk, bordered with wreaths of convolvulus.

They placed no other ornament in her hair than a small sprig of holly with a few red berries on it, or was it a cluster of ivy-berries? I can't say: yet the dame of Chenance, decked out by her fairy friends, was more gay than the loveliest queen of the May. The work was done by the fairy fingers in less than no time; their band playing such lively airs all the while that they could not be slow in their motions.

My senses were overcome with the smell of the fairy odours, the scent of the wall-flowers and honey with which the hollow walls of the house were bursting, and even the honeycombs were hanging down outside the stones under the ivy-leaves, so that they contrived to get much honey without ever killing the bees. The bees might always be seen flying about the house like the birds, and never stung anyone belonging to it.

When I woke up from my doze, I saw that many of the small trade were making wry faces at me, and Betty herself looked as if she wished me to be gone; and, to tell the truth, I was getting rather frightened at the strange doings around me, though we have all heard of such things from our cradles. I soon took my basket and stick, and wished her good afternoon, when I had asked her up to Trove to try our Christmas cheer. Tom is always sure to be here, as he takes the part of the Turkish knight in the squire's guise-dance: he is black enough, to be sure, to pass for any Turk, and my son, the squire's man Jan, as everyone calls him, acts the part of St. George.

When I had passed out and shut the door, for the life of me I could not leave the strange place without taking another peep through the finger-hole and-would you believe it?-when I looked first with my left eye there was nothing strange to be seen: the house was all bright and clean, as it always is; the sun was shining in through the windows on the newly-sanded floor; the robins, wrens and bees are half fairies, I do believe,-they were there flitting about the house and Betty was seated on the chimney-stool mending some of the children's clouts. I winked, and, looking again with my other eye, saw that the room was changed into a banqueting-room, such as I have often seen in my younger days, when old mistress put me with her in the visits she made to a grand place up the country, where some of the squire's rich relations live. But nothing I saw there was so gay as the dwelling of Chenance. The walls were all hung with tapestry, where one might see, as large as life, the pictures of everything on sea and land. There was a grand balcony, with lords and ladies looking down over the railing on the sports below, where the small people were dancing. These left circles of sparkling diamonds behind them wherever they moved on the marble floor. The mistress of the house I saw seated in state under the canopy, casting glances at the door that I didn't much like, and some of her imps looked as if they had a mind to play me a trick.

I tore myself away, glad to get out of the cove. All about the place seemed enchanted. As I crossed over to Kimyal cliff I met many more of the fairy tribe, all bound for the dwelling of Chenance. As I went up the cliff the tide was flowing. One might hear the singing of mermaids above the murmur of the waves, yet it might only have been the wild children of Lamorna sporting on the rocks.

I was soon across the fields through Kimyal, Ragennis, Halwyn, Paul church-town, and out to Choon. I skipped along, went down over Paul hill as lively as a kid, feeling that the drop of French brandy had done me all the good. How true the old saying is, that "a spur in the head is worth two in the heels." I dearly like the truth.

It must have been about four o'clock when I arrived in Penzance. After I had done my marketing, I took a turn down to the new public-house in Market-Jew-street, to have a drink of beer with the piece of Christmas cake I brought in my pocket to eat on the road. The house was so full there was no getting within, and I sat down, with many others, on the long bench placed under the trees opposite the door. The tapster brought us out our drink. There were a number of travellers' and carriers' horses fastened to the mangers placed under the trees below. I conversed with a few old acquaintances, and we wished each other a merry Christmas in some very fair ale, and a little brandy after, that it might not be cold in the stomach.

Old friends are loath to part and I should have stopped much longer if it had not been getting dusk very early. Besides, I thought what a way master would be in if he hadn't the spices brought home in time for making the Christmas ale. I had forgotten some few errands too, and when up among the standings, again looking up such things as I wanted, who should I see but Tom Chenance!He was whipping about as brisk as a bee from standing to stall, picking and pocketing all that pleased his fancy and nobody seemed to notice him. He took hanks of yarn, stockings and cloth from one, shoes and leather, pewter spoons and knives, from another, stuffing all into his wallet together. I could hardly believe my own eyes. I looked and looked again to be sure, before I went up to him and said, "Tom, aren't you ashamed to be here in the dark carrying on such a game?" "Ah, ha!" says he, "is that you, old Joan? which eye can you see me upon?" After winking, it seemed to me that my left eye was bleared, for I could only see him on the right-the one that had been touched with the ointment. I answered, "'Tis plain enough that I can see you on my right eye." Then, looking as if he would look me through, he brought his hand up close to my face; he pointed his finger to my right eye and mumbled out a spell, but I could only catch the words

"*Thou cursed old spy-*
Thou shalt no more see me,
Nor peep nor pry
On that charmed eye."

Then he blew in my face, and, when his blasting breath struck my eye, all the sight was gone; and from that day to this I haven't seen a blink on my blighted eye. I was almost mad with the pain, as I tumbled up and down, calling on the market-women to catch the thief; but they couldn't see the villain. I didn't think of it at the time, but the same devil's salve that caused me to see him made the thief to be unseen.

Some (who were no better than the thief himself) said I was a drunken old baggage and told me to go home the same way as I came. I was so bewildered that I couldn't tell whether I was going towards the Quay or St. Clare, Alwarton or Market-Jew, nor where I was at all, until I again found myself down by the door of the public-house. Then I just took one horn of beer to deaden the pain in my eye, but wouldn't take any more for fear of making my head light.

By good luck I took my bearings right, blind as I was, and steered my course down Voundervoor and over the horse-tracks among the sandybanks, on the Green,-and what a dreary lonely road that is too-not a house as large as a pig's crow beside the road all the way from Voundervoor to Tolcarn, nor a single light to be seen shining from a casement anywhere, except in the windows of a few fishermen's houses in the place they have now named Newlyn. Not being able to see more than half the road I often fell into the ditch on the blind side, and, for fear of missing the track and getting too near the sea, I fell over the low hedge into Park-an-skebbar (the field below the barn belonging to Tolcarn). It was no more than six o'clock then, so the maidens told me who were in the field milking, and the way they were so late was because they finished decking the house with holly and bays and other Christmas greens, before they came out. One of the boys who brought out the hay for the cows put me down as far as Tom Treglown's smith's-shop (you know where it is), a little below the stepping-stones that cross Tolcarn river. Tom took me in and gave me a good glass of new-fashioned, nice cordial called shrub. I would have taken another with all my heart if he had asked me,-it did my stomach so much good; but it is such precious stuff, or he liked it too well himself to ask me take a second glass. However, he was civil enough to lend me a hand to get across the stream. And well for me that he was there to help me; one can never see well where to place one's feet on the stepping-stones when the water is eddying about them in the moonlight, even when one has the best of sight.

My dear Duffy, you may be sure that I was very glad to find myself in Paul and so near home once more. Thinks I to myself I shall be home yet all in good time for the squire to have the spice and things for the Christmas ale: another hour's walk, or less, will bring me home. I hoped that my troubles were over now; but, good Booth, they were hardly begun yet, my dear child, for I didn't reach home for that night. And now I must stop a spell and have a horn to wet my whistle, before I tell you of the narrow escape I had of being carried away bodily by the Old One, more than once, before I reached Trove bottom. And I feel dry whenever I think of it.

I left the smith's house, hoping to reach home in time to get the supper for master and the company that were sure to be at Trove on Christmas Eve, but when I had dragged myself up Paul Hill it was hard work for me to stand up, and I determined, as I passed Choon, that if there was any light to be seen in Rose-an-beagle I would go into Aunt Joney Polgrain's and stop for the night; but when I reached the end of the lane there wasn't a glimmer of light to be seen in the house. Thinks I to myself, dame Polgrain is gone to roost, and, as she isn't the best tempered body in the world, there will be but a cold welcome for me if I disturb her. Then, to rest myself awhile and think whatever I should do to get home, I fell to sit, as I though, on a green bank beside the road, but instead of finding myself on a bank plump down I went in a pit of muddy water, with my heels tossed up higher than my head. By much kicking and scrambling like a toad on his back getting out of a hole, or a beetle kicking himself clear of the dung, I got up to my knees at last, and begged and prayed that I might find an old quiet horse in the lane to have a lift: else I felt (as the weakness of my legs, the sickness of my stomach, and the pain in my eyes, altogether, made my head so light that it was no easy matter for me to stand steady) I should never be able to get home for that night, with my streaming-wet, quilted coats hanging about my legs. I should have been ashamed to go into any decent house then like that of Joney Polgrain, if there had been any light to be seen.

After wringing my petticoats and going on a few steps, there in the ditch (as it seemed in answer to my prayers) stood an old horse, that I took to be uncle Will Polgrain's grey mare (I had seen the beast some place before) hobbled with a halter and eating from the hedge. 'Twas only the work of a moment for me to untie the halter from the legs of the horse and place it over his head and ears, then to mount his back from the hedge. I had to place myself astride. Nobody could sit side-saddle, bare-back, on the lean, razor-backed thing;-as well try to balance oneself without holding fast on the top of a gate or on a pike-staff. The beast, at first, would hardly move one foot before the other, with all the whacking I gave it with my ivory-headed cane over every part within my reach. I might cry gee-up and gee-ho; not a bit the faster would the old thing go, until we got near Trevella, when it pricked up its ears at the cry of some hounds giving tongue (as they often do when out hunting by the moonlight). The beast started to trot going down Trevella lane, faster and faster still, with such rough motion and high action, bump, bump, I couldn't keep my seat without a tight grasp on his tail with my right hand, the halter I held in my left hand and the basket was swinging on that arm: by the time I had the power to sling my cane by the leather loop over my wrist, that I might have the firmer hold of the tail of the horse, or of the devil, or whatever it was, it went like the wind. The more I cried wo-hey! wo-ho! the faster still the thing would go, and it seemed to me, by the time we reached Trevella lane's end, to be grown as high as the tower. Then it would leap across all the turnings and over the corners of the hedges coming into the lane. The wind rose at the same time to a hurricane; mingled with the roaring of the storm was the howling of the dogs and the blast of the huntsman's horn. The thing I was mounted on often rose on end, or plunged in such a way that my heels were sent aloft and my head thrown over the tail, or the pitching of the thing would bring my head down on his shoulder; but, worst of all, my cane hanging down over the rump of the thing, swinging by the thong to my wrist, was sent by the flying legs of the devil's charger all the time wallopping about my head and ears like a flail. Do but think, my dear Duffy, what a picture I must have looked, as we galloped along through Trevella lanes-my best steeple-crowned hat hanging over my back by the strings round my neck, the basket swinging on my left arm, which was dragged out of joint with holding on the halter of the hard-headed brute.

I kept a good hold on the tail of the beast for a long while, but at last, with snorting and blowing, it made a rush over the hedge through bramble and bush into the croft, then back in the lane again and down the road faster and faster-stones and fire flying, the wind howling and getting under my coats, I was so tossed about that I lost my mainstay; that being gone, the wind would every now and then take me up so high that I could barely touch the back of my steed with the high heels of my shoes. On the Clodgey Moor the devil, or dragon, or whatever I was mounted on, took off the road towards the fowling-pool, and people say, you know, that the devil's huntsman and his hounds have often been seen (after hunting Trevella and Mimmis carns) to come down over the moor and vanish in the Clodgey pool. The halter in my left hand was the only thing that now kept me on it, often more standing than sitting, when it galloped round and round the pool. With my stick I hindered it from plunging into the water, and kept on its back until the blast of a whirlwind getting under my coats made me lose the halter and took me up like a feather, towers high. I was kept long hovering in the air and mounting higher and higher until I lost sight of this wicked world. My scarlet cloak spread out on one side, the open skirt of my gown on the other like the outstretched wings of an eagle; true, I never did see one, yet any person (who had chanced to have seen me then) must have taken me for a very uncommon bird, or when coming down one might have taken me for a monster of a kite, and have shot me whilst in the sky beating on against the wind, if the Powers that raised me above this sinful world had not preserved me in a wonderful way from man and devils. Whilst I was flying in the air, with outstretched wings, the black huntsman came down the road over the moor and his hounds came around the pool to drink. The devil's charger (that I was taken from by a miracle that I might escape the old one) ran on to the road, the huntsman blew his horn, sprung on the steed, and when I was dropping slowly down I saw them all-man, horse and hounds-going like lightning down the moors in flashing balls of fire. By a great mercy I came gently down and alighted on a brake of rushes when I again touched the ground. There was plain proof in the sickening smell of sulphur all around that the being who rode the beast away was one of brimstone and not of clay. Through all my riding and flying I kept my basket and stick. The bunch of rushes I was landed on was surrounded with bogs like an island in the sea. In getting off, and wading through the mud on to dry land, my shoes were dragged from my feet; then, barefooted, I hobbled down the moor, keeping on the grass all the way.

It took me a long time to hobble along barefooted from the fowling-pool to the large rock on one side of the brake of thorns, near the horse-track, at the bottom of the moor. I rested a few minutes on the lew side of the rick and was preparing to start once more for home, when I again heard the sounds of the tramp of a horse, the winding of the bugle-horn, and yelping of the hounds. I shook with dread and fear, fell on my knees in prayer that the Lord might again deliver me from the black huntsman, who was now so near that I heard the snorting of his steed. A moment after the sound of the horse's hoofs came within a few yards of the brake and rock; then ceased. I prayed with all my power that the Old One might be deceived of his prey that night. Not hearing any sounds for some time I ventured a look towards the road, and there, at no great distance off, I spied the black huntsman, seated on the same horse with a pillion behind him. We have all heard of the wiles of the devil and the various schemes he takes to tempt poor creatures to their destruction. I prayed that I might not be beguiled by false appearances, nor by any of the allurements of the evil one (who was now come to try the power of his illusions on my poor wearied carcase). As I prayed with all my strength that the devil might not discover my place of refuge, he blew a blast on his bugle-horn, called his hell-hounds together and galloped up the hill. Not a moment longer would I stay on this haunted moor. Not even Sennen Green and Kelynack Downs have a worse name than the Clodgey and the carns around it. I got at last to the gate opening into the North Downs;-the gate is near the river, and just inside the gate is the cow house, where plenty of straw is kept under hand for the young cattle on the downs and moors. I felt as if my bleeding feet would carry me no farther, to save my life. It was as much as ever I could do to crawl into the cow house, and fall down, more dead than alive, among the straw. I was then within a quarter-of-a-mile of home, yet had it been to save my soul I could not have gone a step farther.

Although my pains and sufferings were dreadful, I soon fell into a troubled sleep, with fatigue and weakness, and was again waked up by the tramp of a horse and the barking of dogs, that were soon in the house, all around and treading over me. Grasping my stick, to beat them off, I heard the tramping of boots near the door. "Away with you in the name of the Lord," cried I; and, when I ventured to take my hand from my eyes, there was the squire with a lantern in his hand and the man Jan close behind.

"What have we here? May the devil run away with me," says the squire, "if our old Joan isn't here among the straw dead drunk! When men and boys, with horse and hounds, have been trying to hunt her up in the town and all the country round, during the whole of this blessed night."

"Oh! master," I said, "For the sake of all I have done for you, from your cradle to the time you were booted and breeched, do leave me to die in peace and bury me decent, I beseech you. By all that I have done and suffered for you, from the time you mounted a horse until this the last hour of my life, by the remembrance of all my knitting and spinning, for the sake of all the pies and puddings I have made, and by all that I have done and suffered for you from the time you first mounted a horse until this last blessed hour of my life, my dear master, swear to me, by your horses and hounds and all you love best, that you will let nobody abuse me after I am gone above to my old mistress; but whatever shall I tell her about this wicked world and the bad doings of the people of Buryan?"

"Tell her! Tell who? Hold thy tongue, old fool!" says the squire, after I had made this tender appeal to his best feelings, that might have touched the heart of a bumble bee. Then turning to my unnatural son, he said, "Jan, my dear man, run down to the mill as fast as you can lay feet to ground, for the miller's wheelbarrow, that we pay get out old mammy home before she is frozen to death: tell the miller to bring a flask of brandy and dame Tremellyn to come up quick with some blankets, flour-sacks, or anything that comes to hand to keep the cold from her this frosty morning."

The miller was the first to run up from the mill. "Here, aunt Joan," said he (when the squire raised my head), "take a hair of the dog that bit you; it will do you all the good."

"Oh!" I said, "I have never been the worse of liquor in my life; and as this is the last drop I shall ever taste in this world, I will just take a thimbleful to help me round land comfortable."

By the time I had swallowed the drop of brandy dame Tremellyn had come with blankets and flour-sacks and Jan with the barrow and ropes. They lifted me into the barrow to sit on some straw and covered me over all but my head (I wouldn't have the flour-sacks thrown over my best steeple-crown). The squire and Jan fastened the ropes to the ears of the barrow, to help to get it over the banks and up the hill. Dame Tremellyn held me steady and the miller took the handles. When I found myself once more in the broad green lane among the trees, and trundled along over the smooth bowling-green, I felt that the drop of brandy had saved my life, and when I was seated in the old hall before the blazing fire, eating a bowl of warm wine mixed with eggs and bread that Betty Trevelyan made me take, I should have felt very well but for the remembrance of what I had gone through. Then I told them how I had been served by Tom Chenance, missed my way in consequence; but, most fearful even to think or speak of, how I had escaped twice just by the skin of my teeth, as it were, in a most wonderful way, from being carried off by the Old One, and the last time he came to tempt me to go away-weary worn, and footsore as I was-with a horse and pillion. But, thank the powers, I had the grace to resist all the wiles of the evil one.

Then, to help me overcome my fright (I suppose), they made up a story among them that the steed of Satan that beguiled me was no other than the miller's horse (that no yoke will keep from going over the hedges), which had got into the lane from Trevella croft, where Tremellyn had put it an hour or two before, and fastened with the halter; and the black huntsman and his hounds were no other than my own son Jan and our dogs; that, thinking we hadn't rabbits and hares enough for the Christmas feast, man Jan had taken the hounds and gone off to hunt the crofts about Trevella and Mimmis carns, by the moonlight; that coming down over the moor near the fowling-pool, he had found the miller's horse on the road with the halter under its feet; that then Jan mounted the horse, rode home and finding that I wasn't come home from town, put the saddle and pillion on the miller's horse at once and rode off to town, hoping to meet me on the road. He called at all the houses on the way, to inquire after me, as he said in his impudence that I was like a miller's horse for stopping at every door. Joan Polgrain, in Rose-an-beagle, told him that she had neither seen nor heard of me. At Tom's Smith's shop, by Tolcarn river, Treglown told him that I had passed over the hill many hours before. He was then come back, when the squire, boys and all who had been searching round for me, were going into the cow house. Jan said the story the squire made up was all true, but if the squire tells as big a lie as ever was spoken his man Jan will swear to it, and the miller, the sinful unbelieving wretch, said I was just as much, and no more, in the sky, than his old woman was the other night, when she dreamed that she went up to visit the man in the moon, to know the reason why he had not hung out a better light the other night, for her and the rest of the witches to see how to steer their black ram-cats, and the brooms on which they rode, across the water, to milk the Welshmen's cows. When she awoke there was no putting it out of her head but that she had been aloft all night. She would have me believe that on first staring one night, with the rest from Castle-peak, she (being foremost always) went off with such force that the end of her broom-stick came slap against the sky; the blow made the blue ceiling over this world to ring like a crystal goblet, or a silver bell; and that it continued to ring louder and louder, until it sounded harder than the biggest bell in Buryan tower, when some of the smallest stars fell out with the shock and she came down after them expecting to find them, but they all fell down in the sea somewhere between Penvonlas and Scilly rocks, when their lights were put out and she lost them, except from her hot brains. "I tell you what, Aunt Joan," said the villain of a miller, "It would have been no wonder if my young horse had gone into fits with the fright he must have had to see you fixed astride on his rump, with thy long bony shanks and high-heeled shoes cocked out on each side, your claws stuck fast of his tail, the skirt of your open swing-tail gown and your scarlet cloak flapping about his head and ears, surely he must have thought that something worse than Satan was mounted on his hindquarters when your heavy spiked cane was wallopping about and sticking into the poor brute's legs. Lucky for you old woman," said he, "that you were either blown, thrown, or fell on the brake of rushes; then you went off in a drunken doze and dreamt of flying like a kite or an angel. What a beauty you must have been! You were waked up by the noise of our own Jan, sounding his horn to call in the hounds, saw him mount my nag and gallop down the hill, then you took him, your own son, for the devil. As for the balls of fire they were all in your own hot head, old dear."

"Oh! you liar," I answered, "as if I have not lived long enough in the world and heard enough about such things, not to know the Old One when I saw him; and to speak of him in the way you do is very wicked, you disbelieving sinner."

He told me besides that it was only my vanity and conceit that puffed me up, and sent me flying in the sky. "Old Joan," says he, "do you think yourself of so much importance, that, for your sake, the old gentleman would ever leave his own warm country this cold morning and come tramping from far away, with a horse and pillion, to fetch such a troublesome curious old woman as you are. They would rather never have you among them;-your everlasting meddling would set them all by the ears. And Tom Chenance did no more than right to put out the light of your game eye. You shall have another and a better one made of china, or beautiful clay, that you mayn't see honest people stealing things in the market when they are not near the place. If you came down to the mill with that eye anointed with the devil's-salve you would swear that I, the honest miller, tolled the grist five or six times when I had not put my dish into the sacks more than half so often. I tell you, Joan, all peeping spies only see evil, because they look and wish for that alone; and if they can't see wickedness enough to please them in a natural way they will rub on some of the devil's eye-ointment to make them see as much as they wish for."

I left him go on, but I shall find a chance some day to serve him out, or it's much to me.

I closed my eyes, as I was leaning back in the chimney-corner and seemed to take no heed; but it was a fox's sleep with my eyes closed and ears open. Then I overheard him say to the squire, "If our old Joan, when she was down in the cove, had been treated by Betty to some of the vile, home-distilled, instead of with the pure spirits of France, she would have seen the dwelling of Chenance full of blue devils in place of the pretty innocent small people. Best part of the devils, ghosts and all sorts of apparitions that our old women (whether in petticoats or breeches) see, are merely the vapours of the spirits they take in their drink."

The miller has the impudence to say quite as bad, or worse, to one's face, I know, as he says behind one's back. The squire, poor graceless man, says he is an honest-spoken fellow and my Jan is as bad. I hope I may someday be enabled to forget: then I will forgive them.

After a while the men left the hall and the women got me up to bed. After all my troubles it was no wonder that I soon fell asleep and didn't wake till late in the afternoon: then, taking the twilight for the break of day, I composed myself to sleep again and did not wake up properly, till I heard many voices below singing some of the sweet old carols. I could stay in bed no longer. The squire had been up to church, and, according to his custom, had asked down the singers to give them a treat on Christmas Day in the Evening. Our own-the tenants'-feast was the next day. They began with the carol for Christmas Day in the Morning

"*The first Nowell the angel did say*
Was to three poor shepherds in fields as they lay;
In fields where they lay keeping their sheep
On a cold winter's night that was so deep,
> *Nowell, Nowell, Nowell, Nowell,*
> *Born is the King of Israel.*"

Then the carol of the three ships-

"As I sat down on a sunny bank
On Christmas-day, on Christmas-day,
I saw three ships come sailing in
On Christmas-day in the morning."

I don't remember all this carol, but I shall never forget the sweet music of the last verse-

"O! he did whistle and she did sing,
And all the bells on earth did ring,
For joy that our Saviour he was born
On Christmas-day in the morning."

Next they sang the Cherry-tree Carol-

"Joseph was an old man,
  And an old man was he,
When he married Mary
  In the land of Galilee."

Then "The Seven Sweet Joys of Mary"-

"The first good joy our Mary had," &c.

The last I heard them singing when I fell asleep was the sweet old carol of the "Holy Well," which I like best of all-

"As it fell out one May morning,
  And upon one bright holiday,
Sweet Jesus asked of his mother
  If he might go out to play."

I went to bed early, for Christmas time, and was fast asleep long before they had ceased singing the sweet old carols. All the womenfolk wanted to be early in bed that night, because they had to rise early in the morning of the morrow on Christmas Day; as on that day, long before I was born, the Lovells of Trove have held their Christmas feast for the tenants, when many from a long way away, as well as friends and relations from all over the country, come and remain in Trove over Old Christmas Day. That all might be ready in time for the expected company, the womenfolk had to rise soon after midnight to make the pies, prepare the meat, game and poultry, for roasting, boiling and baking, and to get the great oven, opening into the side of the kitchen chimney, thoroughly heated. By the break of day all the valleys rang and the hills resounded far away, with the sounding of Jan's bugle-horn to rouse the folks of Boleit, Trevider, Kerris, Castallack and all the villages round, to join in the hunting and hare-tracing over the newly-fallen snow. As soon as all the men had left the hall (where they found their breakfast ready before daylight) there was such a fire made in the great chimney of the hall as is only seen there twice a year-at Christmas and the Feast.

The fireplace was filled up all its depth, and from bottom to top, with logs of oak, ash and elm (with bog-turf laid between and piled behind the wood, to keep up a steady fire). By the time the fire was all aglow, and sending out such heat and sweet smoke from wood and turf that one might feel and smell it all over the town, the largest joints were spitted, and the two great spits placed on the hand-irons before the hall fire: an hour or two after, the geese and other small things were placed on the end of the same spits, until our great spits were full from end to end, all the width of the chimney; and many such small things as woodcocks, snipes, plovers, teal and other wild fowl and small game of all sorts and kinds, were placed to roast on the dripping-pans, and turned from time to time. The kitchen chimney, as well as the oven, was all taken up with the pies. Besides all the more common pies-such as those of pigeons and poultry, of rabbits and hares, of mullet and bass, veal and parsley-we had many sorts of savoury herby pies even at that season of the year, from the abundance of beets, round-robins, young nettle-tops, patience docks, sorrel and other new things that are always sprouting in the sunny hedges and slopes of the sheltered spot above the mill-stream that we call the Ladies' Garden, besides many new roots and things that the gardener is getting into the place every year and which gives us plenty of herbs all the time. Then we had the great savoury squab pies, sweet giblet pies and other nick-nacks and sweet pies for the ladies.

As soon as the large things were taken from the oven, cakes and pasties were ready to be put in, the oven continuing hot enough to bake small odds and ends all the day long. The great Christmas puddings had to be boiled in the parlour chimney, every other fireplace being taken up with cooking something or other.

The squire, with some of the elderly hunters and the ladies who went up to the hills and carns to see the chase, returned soon after noon. Then the table was laid, and from that time till long after dark, company after company kept coming home laden with game and as hungry as hounds. As the squire had nobody but myself to take care of him and to look after everything in the house, dear old Madam Pendar came down from Trevider early in the morning to receive the company and to see that everything was in order, and laid out on the hall table with the proper garnishing that the squire likes to see. By the time that all was arranged in the grand old-fashioned style, the squire and visitors from a distance were marshalled into the hall, summoned by the music of the bugle; but, long before the dinner was over, all the grandeur, garniture and style might have gone to the Old One, for what did anyone who had to do with the cooking or eating care about the roasted apples stuck in the mouths of the roasted pigs, or the garlands and sprigs of rosemary and other falderals stuck about this and that? We told the last hunters, who came home when the smoking bowls of punch, tankards of spiced ale and roasted apples were placed on the board, that they might help themselves from the spits, still before the fire-they might cut and come again or go without, for what we cared, as we were quite run down and worn out with so much cooking and serving from long before daylight till after dark.

Then some of the ladies came out of the parlour and turned to with right good will to serve the youngsters, who showed them good sport in the morning, and who would join them in many a lively dance and jolly game before bedtime.

Didn't the old house look grand and glorious that night—decked out with branches of holly, box and bays, with garlands and wreaths of ivy and other greens on window and wall and chimney and board; the painted candles in the great high burnished candlesticks; between the steaming bowls and tankards, piles of apples roasted and raw and heaps of sweet cakes? The light of the candles was little wanted, with the flaming logs of ash and oak that kept the chimney all ablaze.

Then the squire looked to grand and so happy when the stately old ladies came with him and other gentlemen into the hall to see the guise-dance of "St. George and the Turkish Knight," with many other such sports and pastimes as they say are not known up the country. On the whole the best fun we had was in the game of "Burning the Witch." Many a tumble we got from the pole, and hard falls on the stones of the floor, before we could burn the paper effigy of some rank witches and some we could not set ablaze at all.

The young folks enjoyed themselves in playing blind man's bluff in the kitchens, or hide-and-seek in the long dark passages and holes and corners of the old house, where they can kiss in comfort. To tell of all the sports and pastimes we had that night would take all day.

After the guise-dance, Bet of the Mill carne in to sing the old ballads for the dancers in the hall. At the same time the boots of others were stamping to the same tunes on the pavement outside the windows. The older folks called on the miller for some of the drolls that they have heard scores of times before, yet they never tire of hearing the same old stories about the ancient places and people over and over again; and the miller has learned the trick of weaving such things as only happened yesterday (as one may say) into the old drolls, so that they seem ever new and fresh to us: when the squire had pledged the health of the droll-teller and sent him the great goblet brimming with spiced ale, the miller began the droll of the Giant of Nancledrea and Tom, and Jack the Tinker and the High-country folks. Between the different parts of this long old droll, others joined in a three-man song, to give the miller time to drain the cup and breathe awhile.

I was helped to bed long before the story was ended and when the fun was at the highest, that I might rest my weary bones and aching head, which got quite light with the steam and the merest taste of the different sorts of drinks. It was in vain to think of having a wink of sleep, for right under the chamber window more dancing was going on by the moonlight to the tunes they beat up on pewter platters and small brass pans. At last, thank goodness, sometime in the small hours of the morning I heard the cheers for the jolly squire and the healths drunk outside the door from the parting-cup by the few on horseback who were not going to remain over Christmas and I fell asleep in wishing-

A Merry Christmas and Happy New Year to One and All.

A CORNISH GHOST STORY

'YOU Cornishmen think a great deal of your county,' said my old friend Mr. Smith, as we talked of many circuits and many matters.

'Little wonder that we do - where is there one to match it?' was my modest reply.

'Well, for some things I confess you do carry the palm - for hills, for pasties, for pilchards, and last but not least, for ghosts!'

Then the company around the supper table pricked up their ears. Old Mr. Smith, the supernumerary minister, was a treasure of odd tales and strange memories and wonderful experiences in the early days of Methodism.

'Ghosts!' cried everybody.

'Oh, how charming!' said a young lady, turning very pale. 'Do tell us about them, dear Mr. Smith' - and a chorus of plaintive voices echoed the emphasised 'do'.

'Pooh ! Pack o' stuff and nonsense,' observed our host.

'But, Sir, there is much to be said in support of the fact of such supernatural apparitions. Philosophy should not scorn, Sir, but calmly investigate,' replied our sententious superintendent.

'Humbug,' said the host's son, trying to imitate the gruff voice of his father, and looking up for his approval.

'Well, I'm old fashioned enough to believe in them,' said a little old lady, nodding her head, 'and in witches too; and I've lived long enough to see quite as much as most folks.'

'Well, I saw one once,' Mr. Smith remarked gravely, 'and I never wish to see another.'

The company settled down at once, all eager to hear it.

Mr. Smith pulled up his shirt collars, stroked the short fringe of white whisker tenderly, took hold of his chin with the forefinger and thumb, set it on the edge of the many-folded kerchief, and then began very much as if he were preaching a sermon.

'It was in the year of our Lord one thousand eight hundred and thirty-two, in the fall of the year. I was travelling in Bramblecombe Circuit, and was there as the junior preacher, or as it is flippantly termed to-day, the young man. I had been preaching one evening at a little village chapel, and started to walk home the ten dreary miles that lay between me and the circuit town in which I resided. It was very dark and raining heavily. My way lay over Worsedon Moor, one of the loneliest, bleakest, and most desolate places under the sun - that is if the sun ever does shine on Worsedon Moor. It was always mist, or rain, or pitchy dark when I passed it.'

'That lovely Cornish climate!' said my host, slyly winking at me.

I had gone on for two or three miles when I began to be in doubt as to my road. I had surely gone wrong. Yet there was no house anywhere near. I must keep on in the hope of getting to a cottage somewhere. By this time I was wet through and shivering with the cold. And there was the horrible possibility of my wandering about all night, unless indeed I should perish of cold before morning, which seemed not unlikely. However, I pushed on, splashing through puddles and plunging step after step into inches of mud, when suddenly I saw a light. It was shining from a cottage window. I thanked heaven devoutly, and hastened onward. Here I should get direction - perhaps shelter for the night.

I knocked at the door, and immediately I heard someone moving within. The shadows of the window swept round as the candle was moved, and then, holding up the nickering light and looking out into the darkness, an old woman asked, ' Who is it ? '

'If you please ma'am,' I said, 'will you kindly let me come in for a few minutes? I have lost my way, and began to fear that I should be wandering about here all night.'

The old woman held up the light so as to let it fall full on my face, and looked at me out over her heavy spectacles. 'Why, bless me - it is - no, it can't be - but there; it is too, I do believe. Why, you're the new preacher, aren't you my dear ? Why I'm one of your people, you know. Come in, come in. What are you doing out here, this time of night? And like a drowned rat, too! Come in, come in. I'm fine and glad for to see 'you, though you are as wet as a shag, you are.'

In a moment or two more I was seated by the great fireplace, while a single puff of the bellows sent the blaze of the furze leaping and roaring up the chimney as if it bid me a hundred thousand welcomes. Then, to cure any mischief within, there came very quickly a smoking bowl of broth, and soon I was all aglow with warmth. I could not but think of the contrast - inside the cottage all was snug and warm and comfortable; and outside I could hear the rain beating on the window, and the furious gusts roared and thundered and howled as if angry that I had escaped. I knew that the good people with whom I lived would readily suppose that I had sought shelter for the night and not trouble about my absence. So I congratulated myself that I could at least lie down on the hearth and get warmth and rest, if not sleep.

'Well, this is very fortunate that I should find myself in such comfortable quarters,' I said as I set down the basin on the long kitchen table. 'It is very different from what I had anticipated.'

'Oh, my dear life, why I be glad you came. Why, I wouldn't have had you traipsing about upon the downs this time of night, not for anything. There, to think of it too, the pixies up to all sorts of mischief, leading anybody out of the way, and drawing them off to Deadman's Bog ! And with a special spite against parsons, too, as I've heard folks say.'

Of course, in my own mind I ridiculed the idea of pixies and all their tribe; but as there was nothing to be gained by opposing her harmless belief I turned the topic of conversation.

'Well, it certainly is very providential that I should find myself in such comfortable quarters - and with one of our own people too.'

'A member going on for this fifty-five year, Sir, and haven't missed a quarterly ticket all that time. They're in that basin up upon top of the dresser - and I kept the poor dear man's along with them, Sir, till he died - that will be seventeen years come next Michelmas.'

'And what became of them then?' I asked.

'Why, they were buried along with him, of course, Sir. Not that there's any virtue like in it, Sir; but he didn't like for to think of their being all left lying about, and burnt perhaps, so I pasted them upon a sheet of newspaper, and they was buried long with him over in Penrudduck Churchtown. I believe he wouldn't have rested so comfortable in his grave if I hadn't done it.'

'Well,' I said, abruptly coming to the point which I had been trying to reach for some time, 'can you give me a bed?'

The old lady looked up from the long black worsted stocking which she was knitting and laid it solemnly on her lap. She looked cautiously round over her shoulder as if someone were standing in the steep staircase that led to the sleeping apartments. Then in a tone partly of awe and partly of confidence, she whispered hoarsely, 'A bed! Oh, my dear, don't you know about it, then? Haven't you heard tell of it? Why, it is known all over the county I do believe - that Betsy Pengelley's house is haunted! And with a special spite against parsons too, as I've heard folks say.'

'Nonsense - nonsense, my good woman,' I said, in my bravest and cheeriest tone. 'We must not believe all the silly stories we hear. Come now, have you a spare bed in the house?'

'Oh no, my dear minister, it is no good for you to talk - not a ha'porth of good. Spare bed? Yes; and that's the very bed, and that there is the very room where they do walk to. No, I wouldn't put you in there, not for nothing. Why, there wouldn't be an inch of you left in the morning - not enough for a coroner's inquest to sit upon!'

I certainly did wish that I was at home; but I was not nervous - not in the least. Still I felt -

'Creepy like,' put in our host.

'No, not that - but an indefinable sort of a wish that I had not reached that particular house. But I did not show it in the least. 'What is the nature of the apparition then?' I asked, in the same unconcerned tone.

'I don't know what the nature of them is, Sir; but they be uncommon ghastly trade - what I do call, Sir, uncommon ghastly.'

Argument evidently would avail nothing, so I rose for action. 'Come now, my good woman, show me this room.'

Again she looked with frightened eyes at the staircase, and taking the needle from which she had worked off the stitches, she pointed it at me by way of emphasis, and went on, in her hoarse whisper, -

'Tis seventeen year ago, since the poor dear man died. Well, my little granddaughter came down and slept in that there room, and she heard them there awful sounds and saw them there awful sights, as frightened the little maid into fits, and she had them dreadful till she were grow up to be a woman. Oh no my dear, you shan't go in there at all.' And plunging the needle into the stocking, she hurried away at it again, nodding her head and muttering to herself, 'No not for worlds he shan't. And with a special spite against parsons, as I've heard folks say.'

The only chance of success lay in my quiet determination. 'Come now, you have quite roused my curiosity. At least let me look at this wonderful room.' And I took up the candle.

Still muttering that I should only look in, she led me up the creaking stairs. The big lock and the bars that fastened it were thrown back, then pushing her forefinger through a round hole in the door she lifted the latch and there we stood in the haunted chamber. It looked innocent enough. A large, heavy curtained bed seemed to fill it, but as we moved on with the dim light I found that the apartment was long, and that directly opposite the foot of the bed there was a large fireplace, and above it a tall mantelpiece with grotesque carving, and crowned by large, hideous china 'ornaments,' as they used to be called with cruel satire.

The sticks and furze were laid ready for lighting, so stooping down with the candle I said, 'You won't mind my lighting it, will you?' And before an answer came the flames were crackling and shadows danced mysteriously over the bed and on the walls. 'Now I have only one favour more,' I said. 'Will you air the sheets for a little while here, before the fire? I dare say I can set them right when I come up again.' And thinking that I had carried my point I made for the door. Snatching at the candle the old lady followed me hastily and gasped, -

'Oh, you gave me such a turn, Sir, leaving me there all alone - I do always have a neighbour woman in, Sir, to make it up!'

'Oh, if that's it I'll help you,' I said, hastening back and working energetically, thankful to have made matters right thus far.

Then as we sat by the fire below, a chapter from the Testament, a happy talk about it, and a few words of prayer closed the evening there and I rose to retire.

'Oh, I wish you wouldn't - I do sure enough. You'll see something dreadful, I do know you will - for sure and certain.'

'Good night,' I said cheerily, shaking hands with the old woman, 'I shall soon be asleep, and must hope for pleasant dreams.' As I came up the creaking stairs I heard her muttering, 'And with a special spite against parsons, too, as I've heard folks say.'

The candle was out; and I was in bed. I did not like it much, I confess. The wind howled dismally in the chimney. The flickering flames sent dancing shadows all over the room. The floor creaked in a most unaccountable manner. The place smelt all strange and ghostly-like, and I wished with all my heart that I was at home. But I was very wearied and soon, in spite of all my misgivings, I was fast asleep. How long I slept I can't tell - certainly not long when I was awoke by a most hideous and unearthly screech.

I looked up, and found that the fire was still burning with a dull red glare, so that I could faintly see from between the curtains.

There certainly was something!

Something white, too!

It moved noiselessly towards the fire-place - so that I could look down over the foot of the bed and distinctly trace the white outline.

I really was frightened - horribly frightened. The noise I had heard in my sleep, and now this frightful presence standing there with uplifted hands, as if muttering spells and weaving charms there before the fire!

The cold perspiration dropped from my forehead. My jaw fell, and I was paralysed with fright.

My terror became an agony, as the figure turned from the fire and noiselessly glided to the foot of the bed. Then the clothes were lifted and I was conscious that a cold clammy skeleton hand moved over the bed.

Presently it touched my toe.

'Oh!' I screamed.

Then came a voice.

'You be awake then, my dear minister? Why, I thought your feet might be cold, so I brought in a petticoat to wrap them up in, an' keep them warm. I was afraid the creaking old hinge would disturb you, too. I'll grease it if I'm spared till tomorrow. Good night to you, Sir, I hope you won't see nothing.'

As she disappeared I heard her muttering to herself, 'And with a special spite against parsons too, as I've heard folks say.'

There - that was the only ghost I ever saw, but I never want to see another.'

THE TRAGEDY OF SWEET WILLIAM AND FAIR NANCY.

FAR back in old times William, the son of a fisherman, who dwelt at Pargwarra, lived many years - off and on from a boy - in service with a rich farmer in Eoskestal, and courted his master's only daughter, Nancy who, almost from her childhood, loved the young serving-man with a strength of affection beyond her control.

The youngster, being of a roving turn, often went to sea for many months in summer, and although he was then most wanted on the farm, his master always took him back again when sailors were paid off and merchant ships laid up during the stormy winter season. It was his old master's and Nancy's great delight of winter's nights, to be seated with neighbours around the fire and hear William tell of strange things he had beheld on the ocean and in foreign lands; they wondered at what he related of water-spouts, icebergs, and northern lights, of whales, seals, and Laplanders. And they listened with awe and surprise to what he told them of burning-mountains, where he said he had seen, from a distance, the very mouths of hell vomiting clouds of sulphurous smoke, flames, and rivers of fire. And when sailing as near these dreadful regions as anyone dared venture for the heat, and for fear of having their vessel drawn ashore, where all the nails would be pulled from her planks by the load-stone rocks that bordered these lands; of nights, he had heard high overhead, devils shouting, 'the time is come but such and such a one isn't come;' soon after, one would hear doleful cries and behold black clouds of doomed spirits driven to the burning-mountains by troops of demons. He had seen the wreck of Pharaoh's chariots on the beach of the Red Sea, which, he assured them, had retained the hue from which it took its name ever since the Egyptian hosts were slain and overwhelmed, where their bones are still bleaching on the sands.

But all that was easily believed by his simple hearers, and mere nothing to the marvels he related from shipmates' stories when he told them of those bold mariners who had been farther east and seen the Dead Sea across which no bird could fly - how they had plucked from trees that bordered its black waters apples full of ashes that were tempting to the eye; they had touched Lot's wife turned to salt, and brought home some of her fingers; that was often done, he said, for with the next tide's flow they sprouted out again.

The neighbours liked above all to hear him tell about the dusky men and strange women of Levantine lands, and how the latter would shoot loving glances at British tars through peep-holes cut in their thick black cloth veils.

Now William himself was a wonder of perfection, past compare in Nancy's eyes. She admired him for his stalwart form, for his strange adventures on sea and land, and for the rare presents he brought her home. The farmer, too, liked him just as if he had been his own son, yet it never entered his head that his daughter and only child would ever think of the dashing and careless young seaman as her lover.

Yet her mother, more sharp sighted, soon discovered that her fair Nancy was much in love with their serving-man. When William was gone to sea the dame upbraided her with want of proper pride and self-respect till she had fretted her almost to death's door.

'What a fool you must be,' said she, 'to throw yourself away, or to hanker after one so much beneath you, when your good looks and dowry make you a match for the richest farmer's son in the West Country; think if you wed a poor sailor how you will be scorned by all your relations.'

Nancy replied, 'But little care I for relations' reproach or good will, and sink or swim if ever I marry it shall be the man I love who is able to work and win.'

The dame prevailed on her husband, much against his will, however, not to take the sailor to live there when he returned home again; and she - watching her opportunity - slammed the door in his face and told him he should nevermore harbour beneath her roof.

But the father fearing his only child would pine to death, told her and her lover that if he would try his fortune by a voyage to the Indies or elsewhere for three years, when he returned, poor or rich, if he and Nancy were in the same mind, they might be wedded for all he cared.

That being agreed on, William got a berth in a merchant-man bound for a long voyage, took friendly leave of his old master, and the night before his ship was ready to sail he and Nancy met, and he assured the sorrowing damsel that in three years or less she might expect him to land in Pargwarra with plenty of riches, and he would marry at home or fetch her away and make her his bride. According to the old verses he said -

' Down in a valley, love, where three streams unite,

I'll build thee a castle of ivory and diamonds so bright.

That shall be a guide for poor sailors of a dark stormy night.'

They vowed again and again to be constant and true; with their hands joined in a living spring or stream they broke a gold ring in two between them, each one keeping a part. And to make their vows more binding they kindled, at dead of night, a fire on the Garrack Zans (holy rock), which then stood in Roskestal town-place, and joining their hands over the flame, called on all the powers of heaven and earth to witness their solemn oaths to have each other living or dead. Having plighted their troth with these and other ancient rites - that romantic lovers of old regarded as more sacred than a marriage ceremony - they said farewell, and William went on his way and joined his ship.

Three years passed during which the old dame had done her utmost to persuade her daughter to become the wife of some rich farmer - for true it was, as she said, Nancy might have had her choice of the best - yet coaxing and reproaches were powerless to shake the maid's constancy. When three years and many months were gone without any tidings of William, she became very melancholy - perhaps crazy - from hope deferred, and took to wandering about the cliffs in all weathers, by day and by night.

On the headland, called Hella Point, which stretches far out west of the cove, there is a high over-hanging rock almost on the verge of the cliff, which shelters, on its southern side, a patch of green sward, mostly composed of cliff-pinks; this spot used to be known as Fair Nancy's bed. There she would pass hours by day, and often whole nights, watching vessels that came within her sight, hoping to see her lover land from every one that hove in sight, and to be the first to hail him with joyful greetings in the cove. Her father and the old fisherman - anxious for William's return - treated her as tenderly as a shorn lamb, and often passed long nights with her there; at length the poor maiden had to be watched and followed for fear that in her night wanderings she might fall over the cliff or drown herself in a fit of despair.

One moonlight winter's night, when in her chamber indulging her grief, she heard William's voice just under her window, saying, 'Sweetheart, awaken and come hither, love; my boat awaits us at the cove, you must come this night or never be my bride.'

'My sweet William come at last, I'll be with you in an instant,' she replied.

Nancy's aunt Prudence, who lodged in the same room, heard William's request and his sweetheart's answer; looking out of the window she saw the sailor, just under, dripping wet and deathly pale. An instant after - glancing round into the chamber, and seeing Nancy leave it - she dressed, in all haste, and followed her. Aunt Prudence, running down the cliff lane at her utmost speed, kept the lovers in sight some time, but couldn't overtake them, for they seemed to glide down the rocky pathway leading to Pargwarra as if borne on the wind, till they disappeared in the glen.

At the fisherman's door, however, she again caught a glimpse of them passing over the rocks towards a boat which floated off in the cove. She then ran out upon the How- as the high ground projecting into the cove is called - just in time to see them on a large flat rock beside a boat when a fog, rolling in over sea, shrouded them from her view. She hailed them but heard no reply.

In a few minutes the mist cleared away, bright moonlight again shone on the water, but the boat and lovers had disappeared.

Then she heard mermaids singing a low sweet melody, and saw many of them sporting on the water under Hella; that was nothing new, however, for the rocks and caverns bordering this headland were always noted as favourite resorts of these death-boding sirens, whose wild unearthly strains were often, before tempests, to be heard resounding along Pedn-Penwith shores.

By daybreak the old fisherman came to Poskestal and told the farmer that he hoped to find his son there, for, about midnight he saw him at his bedside, looking ghastly pale; he stayed but a moment, and merely said, 'Farewell father and mother, I am come for my bride and must hasten away,' when he vanished like a spirit. It all seemed to the old man uncertain as a dream; he didn't know if it were his own son in the body or a token of his death.

In the afternoon, before they had ceased wondering and making search for Nancy, a young mariner came to the fisherman's dwelling, and told him that he was chief officer of his son's ship, then at the Mount with a rich cargo from the Indies, bound for another port; but put in there because his son - her captain - when off Pargwarra, where he intended to land last night, eager to see his native place, went aloft, and the ship rolling he missed his grip on the shrouds, fell overboard and sank before any assistance rendered.

All knew then that William's ghost had taken Nancy to a phantom boat, and a watery grave was the lovers' bridal-bed. Thus their vows of constancy, even in death, were fulfilled, and their sad story, for a time, caused Pargwartha to be known as the Sweethearts' Cove, and some will have it that the old Cornish name has that meaning.

THE SMUGGLERS OF PENROSE

WHAT remains of the old mansion of Penrose, in Sennen, stands on a low and lonely site at the head of a narrow valley; through which a mill-brook winds, with many abrupt turns, for about three miles, thence to Penberth Cove. So late as one hundred years ago, it was one of those antique, mysterious looking buildings, which most persons regard with a degree of interest that no modern structure inspires; the upper story only - with its mullioned windows, pointed gables, and massive chimney-stacks - was just seen over the ivy-covered walls of courts and gardens that surrounded it.

There was, however, a certain gloomy air about the ruinous walls and neglected gardens embowered in aged trees, which might have conduced to such unaccountable stories of apparitions and other unnatural occurrences, as were said to have taken place there.

Some three or four centuries ago, it was the property and residence of an ancient family of the same name; little more is known of these old Penroses than what can be gathered from wild traditions related by the winter's hearth. The following among many others were often recounted by old folks of the West.

About three hundred years ago, the owner of Penrose was a younger son who had been brought up to a seafaring life, which he continued to follow till his elder brothers died unmarried and left him heir to the family estate; then, preferring a life on the wave, he kept a well-armed, fast-sailing, craft for fair-trading, or what is now called smuggling; she was manned with as brave a crew as could be picked out of the West Country; most of them are said to have been the Squire's poor relations. A favourite cousin, called William Penrose - who had been his shipmate for years - was captain of the merry men all.

The Squire often took trips to France and other places, whence his goods were brought, and it is said that in his days Penrose crew were never concerned in any piratical jobs; though we know that about that time smuggler, privateer, and pirate, meant very much the same thing, whilst the two latter were then interchangeable terms.

Penrose and his seamen passed but little time on shore except in the depth of winter; yet the board in his hall was always furnished with good substantial fare and the best of liquors, free for all comers.

Over a few years, when the good man was left a widower, with an only child - a boy about seven or eight - he seemed to dislike the very sight of land, for then, even in winter, with his little son, his cousin William, and two or three old sailors, he would stay out at sea for weeks on end; leaving, as usual, the care of his farms and household to the care of a younger brother and an old bailiff.

In returning from one of these trips, in a dark winter's night, their boat struck on Cowloe and became a wreck. The Squire swam into Sennen Cove with his boy but in endeavouring to save his crew got drowned himself.

The only remaining brother, known as Jan of Penrose, constituted himself sole guardian of the heir and master of the place and property.

Now this Jan hated all whom his late brother favoured; and in consequence of his ill-will William Penrose left the West Country - for the sea it was supposed - but whither he wandered was unknown, as no tidings of him were received in the West.

The new master, however, soon got a large smuggling craft and manned her with a crew who cared but little what they did for gold or an exciting life; being well-armed they feared nothing that sailed the ocean.

Jan of Penrose never went to sea; but gave the command to a wretch - known to have been a pirate - who was cast on

Gwenvor sands from his ship wrecked in Whitsand Bay, on the night that the good Squire Penrose was drowned.

This pirate-smuggler and his desperate crew boarded many a rich merchant-man going up Channel, from which they appropriated whatsoever they pleased, and sent all who opposed them to the other world by water.

There was no Preventive Service then, to be any check on our free trade. If Revenue Cutters came near our western land, their crews dreaded to fall in with Cornish fair-traders more than our smugglers feared the King's men. As for riding officers they would ride anywhere else rather than on the cliff, when beacon fires blazed from the cairns of dark nights to guide fair-traders' boats into the coves.

When the rich goods and plunder were landed the jolly crew would give themselves credit for being valiant privateers, and as such be much renowned by simple country folks, and their plunder passed as lawful prize.

People came from all over the country to purchase the goods, safely stowed in vaults and other hiding places about Penrose; and in winter the crew spent much of their time there in drunken rioting with all the reckless youngsters of the neighbourhood.

After the good Squire was drowned his brother appeared to show every kindness to the orphan heir; yet it was remarked that the child seemed instinctively to avoid his uncle and the captain, who consorted much together when the smugglers were ashore.

Whenever the boy could elude the old steward's vigilance he would go away alone to the rocks in Sennen Cove where his father was drowned, or shut himself up for hours in his father's bed-room, or wander about other parts of the gloomy north wing, which was almost in ruins and seldom entered by other inmates.

One winter's day, the ground being covered with snow, Penrose's people and many others of the neighbourhood joined for a wolf-hunt. Traditions say that in those times terrible havoc was often made on flocks by these fierce beasts, and that children were sometimes carried off by them when hard pressed with hunger.

Neither John Penrose nor the captain went to the chase; when at night the game-laden hunters returned and blew their bugle-horns, they remarked with surprise that the young heir - who was a general favourite - did not, as was his custom, come into the court to meet them. The boy was sought for in every place where it was thought he might have strayed. His uncle seemed to be much distressed, and continued the fruitless search until it was surmised that the child must have missed his way in returning from Sennen Cove, wandered out under Escols Cliff, there got drowned by the flowing tide, and carried out to sea on the ebb.

After this, Jan of Penrose, having all his own, became more riotously debauched than ever. His gang took a somewhat strange aversion to their captain, so he left and was no more seen in the West.

The tapestry chamber and all the northern wing was shut up, or unoccupied, as it had the reputation of being haunted. None of the servants nor even the devil-may-care smugglers would venture into it after night-fall, when unearthly shrieks would be heard there, and strange lights seen flashing through the casements till near morning. Lights were also often seen in an orchard just below the town-place when no one was there.

These unnatural occurrences, however, put no check to the excesses of Penrose's band and the lawless castaways who joined them. By way of variety to their fun, they frequently disguised themselves and made nocturnal excursions to some village within a few miles, where they would alarm the quiet folks in the dead of night, by discharging their fire-arms in a volley; and make a bonfire of a furze-rick, out-house, or thatched dwelling.

The poor villagers in their fright would mistake these wretches for outlandish people, come again to burn and pillage as in days of old.

They were all the more ready to think so because about this time the Spaniards had great fondness for roving round the western coasts, and often did much damage in defenceless places; it was in Jan Penrose's time, too, that a few Dons, high by day, put off from a galley in Whitsand Bay, landed on Gwenvor Sands, and destroyed Velan-dreath Mill. To return to the Penrose crew, at the height of the fright and confusion they would carry off such young women as they had before agreed on; the gallants would take their fair-ones before them on horseback to Escols Cliff or the hills, where they would be left alone by daybreak, to find their way back afoot. Having carried on this sport a long time with impunity, they became so bold at last as to make an attack on Buryan Churchtown; fortunately, however, Buryan men were appraised of their intentions in time to be armed and ready to give them a warm reception; in short they lay in wait for the smugglers, drove them all into a vacant place near the cross in Churchtown, and there surrounded them; when thus hemmed in the band fought desperately, and till nearly every man of them was killed or disabled they continued shouting to each other, 'cheer up comrades, die one, die all, and die we merrily;' and so many of them met their end in this encounter that the Penrose band was soon after broken up.

One night of the following Christmas, whilst a large company was assembled at Penrose, keeping high festival after a day's hunt, loud knocking was heard at the green-court door, and soon after a servant conducted into the hall an elderly wayfaring man who requested a night's shelter from the snow-storm.

John Penrose received the wanderer with hospitable courtesy; and charged his steward, the old bailiff, to provide him with good cheer; the guests continued their glee and paid but little attention to him, for begging homeless pilgrims were all too plenty here at that time.

The company was also entertained by professional droll-tellers and ballad-singers; persons of that class were then - and long after continued to be - received, as substitutes for minstrels, in gentlemen's houses of the humbler sort.

The stranger, however, regarded the company with attention, and noticed that the master of Penrose looked wretched and haggard amidst all the merriment. His scrutiny was interrupted by the steward who conducted him to another room where a well furnished board, beside a blazing fire, awaited him.

The stranger having refreshed himself, told the old steward how he had just returned from a long pilgrimage in foreign lands, and had seen many places spoken of in miracle-plays, which were acted in the Plan-an-Gware at St. Just, and how he had that morning arrived at Market-jew on board an eastern ship that traded there for tin.

He also said that he once had friends in the West Country; whether they were alive or dead he knew not, but hoped to obtain some tidings of them on the morrow.

The wanderer's voice seemed familiar to the old steward, and recalled former times; but, before they had time for more discourse, they were invited to return to the hall and see a guise-dance, which was about to commence.

The stranger seemed interested in the quaint performance of "St. George and the Turkish Knight." A droll-teller in his character of bard, took the part of chorus; explained the intent of coming scenes; instructed and prompted the actors as well.

The play being concluded and the players well rewarded by the wayfarer, he withdrew and told the steward that he felt weary after his long walk through the snow and would be glad to lie down; if all the beds were occupied, he could repose, he said, in a settle by the fireside, for a few hours only, as he intended to leave early in the morning.

The old man replied that he feared any other accommodation in his power to offer was not such as he might desire, - although the house was large, with ample bed-rooms for more guests than it now contained - because a great part of the northern end was shut up for a reason that the inmates did not like to talk about. Yet as he believed the pilgrim to be a prudent man, who was, no doubt, learned in ghostly matters, he was glad to unburden his own mind and have his visitor's counsel, with his prayers for the repose of the unquiet spirits that disturbed the place.

Then he told how many of the upper rooms, though well furnished, were unused and falling to ruin on account of the un- natural sounds and sights before mentioned. To which the stranger answered that as he had a mind at ease he had no reason to dread any ghostly visitants; if the steward would conduct him to a room in the haunted wing he did not fear for his rest.

The old steward, taking a lamp, led the way to the tapestry chamber - being the best room in that part of the mansion. A faggot of dry ash-wood - already laid in the large open fire-place - was soon in a blaze, and the room well aired and somewhat comfortable.

The old man brought in bread, meat, and wine, that the guest might take more refreshment during the night, and supply his wallet in the morning if he started before breakfast. After returning with more wood and bog-turf to keep in the fire, he bade the guest good-night, sweet rest, and pleasant dreams.

After the old steward had retired from the dreaded room, its occupant was in no haste to rest himself on the large stately looking bed; but seemed never weary of examining the old portraits and quaint figures in the arras (which might have been intended for portraits too), the massive oak furniture with bold, grotesque, carvings, ancient armour, coats of mail, and other interesting objects, which were suspended from the walls, or in hanging presses, with all of which he appeared familiar; so that it was near midnight when he sat down in the long window- seat.

The storm had ceased and a full moon, shining on newly fallen snow, made it almost as light as day. He opened the casement and looked into the court, where he saw a company of young men and women passing out singly and in silence.

The visitor, being well acquainted with West Country customs, knew - as this was twelfth night - that the object of this silent procession was to work some of the many spells, usually practised at this time, for the purpose of gaining a knowledge of their future destiny with respect to what they regarded as the most important of all events - marriage and death.

So great was the desire of many young people to obtain an insight of what the future had in store for them, that they often practised singular rites, - still well-known in the West, - which are probably vestiges of ancient magic ceremonials connected with divination.

This night, however, the young peoples' intention was simply to gather ivy leaves and pull rushes; by the aid of which, with fire and water, they hoped to discover who would be wedded, and with whom, or buried before the new year was ended. There are many instances of predictions, with regard to the latter event, conducing to accomplish their own fulfilment, from their effects on people of melancholy temperament.

The pilgrim had not sat long, looking out of the open casement, when he saw the company of young men and maidens come running back, apparently in great fright. The doors were all immediately slammed to, the noisy mirth and music suddenly ceased in the hall. The house, in a few moments, was shrouded in thick fog; all was still as death about the place for some minutes, then a noise was heard like the distant roaring and moaning of the sea in a storm.

These ocean sounds seemed to approach nearer and nearer every instant, until the waves were heard as if breaking and surging around the house. In the wailing wind was heard a noise of oars rattling in their rowlocks for another instant; then as of the casting of oars hastily into a boat. This was followed by the hollow voices of the smugglers, drowned with the old Squire, hailing their own names, as drowned men's ghosts are said to do when they want the assistance of the living to procure them rest.

All this time the green-court appeared as if filled with the sea, and one could hear the breakers roaring as when standing on a cliff in a storm. All the buildings and trees surrounding the mansion disappeared as if sunk into the ground.

At length the surging of waves and other sounds gradually died away until they were only heard like the 'calling of cliffs' before a tempest.

The steward had told the stranger of these noises and appearances, which had become frequent of late, to the great terror of the household; but he gave little heed to the old man's tales, thinking that such visions were merely the creations of weak brains diseased by strong potions.

'Tis said that when the young folks reached the outer gate of the avenue, near which they would find the plants required for their spells, all keeping silence and taking care not to look behind them - as this or speaking would spoil the charm - a female, who was a short distance ahead of the others, saw what appeared to be the sea coming over the moors before a driving fog. She ran shrieking to join her companions, who also saw the waves fast approaching - rolling, curling, and breaking on the heath. They all ran up to the house with the utmost speed; and some who had the courage to look behind them, when near the court door, saw the curling breakers within a few yards of them; and a boat, manned with a ghostly crew, came out of the driving mist as they rushed into the house; and, not daring to look out, they saw nothing more.

The weary wayfaring man, having a clear conscience, feared nothing evil in what appeared to him an unaccountable mystery, even in that time of marvels; and, having said his prayers, he committed himself to good spirits' care.

The brave man was rather soothed than alarmed by a plaintive melody, until there was a change in the harmonious strains, which grew more distinct; and mingled with them were the tones of loved and once familiar voices, calling, 'William Penrose, arise and avenge the murder of your cousin's son! '

Casting a glance towards the window - where the sound came from - he saw just within it the apparition of a beautiful boy in white raiment. A light which surrounded it showed the countenance of the lost heir of Penrose. At the same time the room was filled with an odour like that of sweet spring flowers.

The pilgrim, William Penrose, spoke to the spirit and conjured it, according to the form prescribed by Holy Church, to speak and say what he should do to give it rest.

The apparition, coming nearer, told how he had been murdered by the pirate-captain of the smugglers, on the grand hunting day; and how his uncle had given the pirate a great quantity of gold to do the bloody deed - that he had been buried in the orchard under an apple-tree, that would be known, even in winter, by its blasted appearance, - that the murderer was then in Plymouth, keeping a public-house, the situation of which was so plainly described by the spirit that William Penrose would have no difficulty in finding it, and bringing the murderer to justice by means of such proofs of his crime as would be found beneath the blasted tree.

Moreover he told William that the spirits knew he was gone on a pilgrimage for their repose; and that they all, through him, sought his aid to enable them to rest in peace.

William Penrose, having promised to perform all according to the wishes of the departed, heard music again and the spirit gradually disappeared in a cloud of light. Then the weary man sunk into sound repose from which he only awoke at break of day.

His cousin, the good Squire, had also appeared to him in a dream, and told him that concealed in the wainscot, beneath a certain piece of tapestry, he would find a secret cabinet, in which was preserved a good store of gold and jewels for the infant heir; and that the key of this hidden treasury was behind a leaf of carved foliage which ornamented the bed head. He was told to take what money he required for his journey and to keep the key.

He found everything as indicated in his dream.

Jan of Penrose had often sought for this private recess - where heirlooms and other valuables were concealed, and only made known to the heir when of age, or to a trusty guardian, if a minor - but he was deterred from further search by such an apparition as made him avoid the chamber, and of which he would never speak after his fearful fright was past.

The pilgrim arose and requested the old steward to accompany him a short distance on his journey.

Before they parted the stranger revealed himself, to the old man's great delight, to be the long-lamented William Penrose; told him that he was about to undertake a long journey for the repose of the dead; that he would return when he had accomplished his mission; and bade the steward adieu, without speaking of the apparition or the cause of disturbances in the mansion.

William Penrose, having arrived in the ancient town of Plymouth, and entered the mean public-house to which he had been directed by the apparition, saw the person he sought lying stretched by the fireside in a squalid apartment that served for kitchen, guest-chamber and sleeping room.

The former pirate-captain looked like a deserter from the churchyard (as we say); the face of this child-murderer was the colour of one long in the tomb; with but little signs of life except in the lurid glare of his sunken eyes.

William Penrose with much difficulty induced the 'sad-looking' object to converse; and, after a while, led him to talk of the West Country, then of Sennen. From that the pilgrim spoke of Penrose, and asked him if he knew, in Penrose orchard, a certain apple-tree, which he pointedly described. He had no sooner mentioned it than the inn-keeper exclaimed, 'I am a dead man.'

The miserable wretch begged the pilgrim to have mercy on him and listen to his confession, in which he declared he was driven to commit the murder by his evil spirit that made him dislike the child, because he had long hated his parents, more than from any love of gold given him by Jan of Penrose, to remove the only obstacle to his possession of the estate.

William Penrose - who was still unknown to the inn-keeper - wondered what cause of ill-will he could ever have had against the good old Squire or his wife, until the former pirate told how he was the prodigal son - long supposed dead- of an ancient, respectable, but poor family, whose ancestral seat was within a few miles of Penrose. How, almost from his childhood, he had long and truly loved, and as he trusted, had his love returned by the lady who became the wife of Squire Penrose, how that he had left his home in St. Just on a desperate privateering expedition, in hopes of soon gaining sufficient riches to make the lady's parents regard him with favour, how, whilst he was returning with gold enough to buy the parish, Penrose had wooed and won the lady - his first and only love, for whom he had toiled and suffered every hardship during many years.

He also related how when he came home so altered, by the burning suns of the Spanish Main, that his nearest relatives knew him not, and found out the ill return his lady-love had made him, that his only solace was the hope of revenge.

Some of the gold that he had sweat blood to gain, for the sake of the faithless woman, was spent on a fast sailing craft, which might pass for a merchantman, privateer, or pirate, as she was all in turn during a few years that he roamed the British seas.

The vessel was manned with a desperate crew, most of them his old comrades, who would do anything to please him. The design he had formed, more through hate than love, was to carry the lady off to some foreign land.

A year or so after his return he landed one night in Whitsand Bay, accompanied by a great part of his well-armed crew, who made their way towards Penrose, where he learned before their arrival, that his design of carrying off the lady was frustrated by her having been laid in the grave a few days earlier.

After this he wandered over sea and land by turns, caring nothing what became of him, until cast on Gwenvor Sands - poor and naked - as his ship foundered in deep water, when all but himself were drowned; and, as bad luck would have it, he reached the shore on some loose part of the wreck.

The worst portion of his story from this time is already told; but no one can tell, as he related, how the desire of gold - to enable him to recommence his roving life, far away from the hated sight of the land and everything else that recalled a remembrance of his blighted youthful hopes - maddening drink, and a wicked heart, farther irritated by Jan Penrose, made him murder the child that he would have given a hundred lives to restore before he received the uncle's bloody gold.

Since then he had never a moment been free from remorse. He wished for death, but feared to die. If he drank himself mad, that only increased the horror of his thoughts.

He had scarcely finished his sad tale when William Penrose revealed himself to be the well-remembered playmate of the wretched man's innocent youth and he had only time to beg Penrose to bestow in alms his ill-gotten store, for the scarcely hoped for mitigation of future punishment, when he breathed his last.

When William Penrose returned to Penrose and made himself known, to the great joy of old servants and others, he found that what was thought to be merely the gloomy and morose temper of its master frequently made him shun all society and wander about the hills or cliffs and other solitary places, for days and nights together.

No one either loved, feared, or cared enough about the surly man to pay him any regard. He was absent then in one of his melancholy moods, and William with the steward, aided by other old trusty servants, removed the child's remains from beneath the blasted tree to Sennen churchyard; and out of respect to the honourable old family, little was said or known about the sad occurrence.

Jan of Penrose was no more seen alive in the old mansion, for the same night that his nephew's remains were buried in consecrated ground, he hanged himself in the malt-house; and he haunted it long after.

Following the spirit's injunction William Penrose had still to find and remove the bodies of the old Squire and his crew. Now it was supposed that they were 'sanded' - that is sunk in the moist sand and covered by it during a flowing tide - near Gwenvor Cove, because corpse-lights had frequently been seen, and the drowned sailors had been heard there 'hailing their own names,' as they are still accustomed to do when requiring aid of the living.

Next day Penrose and others found the bodies of the old sailor-squire and his crew near the place where fishermen had heard the 'calling of the dead,' and their remains were laid to repose, with all holy rites, in an ancient burying-ground near Chapel Idne, where the wind and waves sing their everlasting requiem in music they loved well when alive : -

'Pie Jesu, Domine,

Dona eis requiem.

Amen.'

William Penrose, now heir-at-law of the bartons of Penrose, Brew, and other farms in the West Country, - disliking to live in the place connected with such melancholy events - gave up his rights of heirship to another branch of the family; resumed his pilgrim's staff; and was supposed to have died in the Holy Land.

THE LADY OF THE SILVER BELL

THIS story concerns a period, when a certain Baron was Lord of the ancient castle at Tintagel and lived there in much splendour and state.

This great Baron had only one child, a daughter, who was as fair as a lily, and when she turned her head, her neck moved with the grace and beauty of the swan; at least that is how she was described by the old harpist in his songs, as, every feast day, he gladdened the halls of Tintagel with the thrilling notes and full chords of his harp. She was commonly called Serena, on account of her generally placid demeanour; and as her father was very fond of seeing her dressed in white and silver, because he thought she looked prettiest when so attired; she was not infrequently called the silver lady.

Judy, her nurse declared, that, when the child was in the cradle, she had been blessed by the Pixies; and it was that which made her look so fair and beautiful, and caused her to be so lucky in everything she did.

'But woe be to her,' the old gossip would add, when she said this, 'if my lady Serena should offend the Pixies; for, like us mortal sinners, they will often most hate where they have most loved; and especially if they be jealous or offended.'

Although her mother died when she was an infant, Serena received a very good education; for her nurse taught her so well how to work with the needle, that all the finest tapestry hangings in the castle were said to be in part made by her. The old minstrel instructed her in playing the harp and she often sang to it many a Cornish ballad or ditty; and, above all, Father Hilary had well disciplined her in her religious duties. She had given him a promise that she would never be absent from church at the ringing of the vesper bell; never, she said, unless prevented by sickness, would she be tempted to stay

169

away when that bell was calling her to prayers, no matter what. She gave this promise to Father Hilary so seriously, that he, as well as the nurse, assured her, if ever she broke it, the good spirits who were her guardians would fly away from her, and leave her exposed to injury from the bad ones. Serena said, in reply, 'No music was so sweet to her ears as the vesper bell.'

But though the Baron's daughter had so many good qualities, she had, I am sorry to say, some very great faults. She was excessively vain and fond of dress, and at times sadly whimsical and unpredictable. When she grew up to womanhood, her father wanted her to marry one of the gallant young knights who came to the castle; but such was her vanity, she thought that none was good enough. Among them was a very gentle and amiable youth, who was so comely and graceful, that everybody said how happy she would be as his wife. And the old nurse declared that, from the dreams she had about him, and his having first been brought to the sight of her young lady, by the sounds of sweet music, which seemed to float in the air and to guide his steps to Tintagel, at the very moment Serena was issuing from the castle gates, she was quite sure it was the Pixies, and nothing but the Pixies, who thus led him along to give him, as a very great favour, to Serena for a husband. Serena at first appeared to like him well, and he came very often to the castle; but at length she changed her mind, tossed her head, disappointed him, and said that neither he nor any other of her father's friends, were handsome enough to please her; and on a whim, she declared that she would never marry unless she could meet with a young prince who was handsomer, and dressed better, and played on the lute sweeter, than any one she had ever yet seen or heard.

Her old nurse sighed as she listened to all this, and said, 'O my dear young lady, do not talk so! Beware what you say. You have behaved ill and whimsically to that poor young gentleman, whom everybody loved; he was so good and kind.

Depend upon it, the Pixies will take their revenge one of these days for the manner in which you treated him, or I don't know them or their doings. The only way to save yourselves from their spite, is to be very penitent for your fault; and to be mindful of your promise to Father Hilary. For if you go wrong again, the evil spirits may take advantage of your folly, sadly to mislead and deceive you; and I should break my old heart if any harm happened to my dear young lady, whom I have nursed in these arms from the hour she was born.'

Serena paid little heed to this good advice, but soon after indulged in such extravagance and gaiety, in so much dancing and singing, that Father Hilary interfered, and strictly enjoined her, as a sort of penance for spending her time so idly, to repair alone every day for one month to come, to a little chapel which stood near St. Nectan's Kieve, which we now call St. Nectan's Glen, and to be sure, according to her promise, always to enter within its doors before the ringing of the vesper bell had ceased.

St. Nectan's Kieve was three miles and a half from Tintagel, a long and weary way, and over a difficult road; and Serena now and then went on horseback. Yet walking through such rough paths was a sort of penance, to please old Hilary, who was rather cross-grained and crabbed, and had no pity for her poor feet, she more frequently walked than rode.

One day, Serena set out early on foot, as she was determined not to be hurried in her walk. She was dressed in a long grey cloak, and upon her head she wore a little grey cap made of cloth; a scallop shell was seen in front of it, to show that she was going on a sort of pilgrimage. As she put on her cloak, her nurse gave her a caution to let nothing stay her by the way, but to go on straight to the chapel, to enter before the bell had ceased ringing, come straight home, for, said the good old woman, 'those who allow anything they meet with to delay them when they are going to prayers, are sure to lay themselves open to the power of those wicked spirits that I told you of before, they are sure to be punished for it.'

Serena took leave of her aged counsellor with repeated promises to mind what she said. She passed the castle gates in a somewhat hurried manner, for fear of meeting Father Hilary, as she did not like to be lectured by him on her way. With a quick step she also passed the village of Trevenna. As she began to ascend the high ground beyond it, she slackened her pace, and looked back upon Tintagel, which now opened with all its grandeur of castle and cliff upon the view. She had never so attentively observed it as on this day; and, she could not tell why, but she then gazed upon it with a melancholy interest.

It was indeed a fine sight, and whilst the walls and towers of her father's ancient dwelling were lit up with a flood of light, the rock called Long Island, was in complete gloom from the overshadowing clouds. This rock, wild, lofty, broken, close in shore, though surrounded by the waves, was said to be peopled, and especially after nightfall, by sea-gulls and spirits. Serena now, therefore, looked upon it in its sombre hue with a secret sense of dread. Nor was it without a shudder that as she turned to continue her walk she saw a solitary magpie pacing up and down on the very road she had to cross. She did not like the evil sign, and she thought that she would take a shorter way, and search out the way that the country people sometimes took in going to chapel.

But Serena was soon bewildered and eventually found herself on a strange rough road over a field that descended as precipitously as the roof of a house to the bottom of a ravine, beautifully clothed with wood. She could hear the running of water and soon came in sight of a stream that ran rapidly under a vast number of trees. This she crossed and still advanced. She now perceived some overhanging rocks, and on the hill above these stood the little chapel. She had not advanced very far, when she heard the vesper bell. Mindful of her promise she determined to retrace her steps as speedily as possible, and no longer linger, though in so lovely a scene.

But at that very moment she heard strains of the most enchanting music. Nothing earthly seemed to mingle with those sounds. 'O Serena! Serena, quickly turn, hark to the vesper bell.' She fancied that a voice above the rocks spoke these words. But, alas! she neglected the friendly warning. She looked this way, that way, up the ravine, among the trees, and could see no one; whilst every step she advanced, the music of the unseen musician appeared to move on before her. 'I will but tarry a few minutes to see who it is plays thus sweetly, and where the sounds come from,' said Serena, 'I shall yet reach the chapel yonder, before the bell has done ringing.'

She now continued descending the difficult and winding path, which turned sharply round among rocks that peered above her head in the most fantastic forms; the roots of the trees clung to them in all directions. So narrow had the path become between the rocks and the stream, that it scarcely afforded room to pass; and as the stones were slippery with moss and damp, and here and there the arm of a tree crossed close above the head, to pass along was both precarious and dangerous.

Again did Serena listen, and still could she hear, even above the sounds of the rushing waters, the vesper-bell. She now in good earnest determined to turn back. But at that moment, such a strain of sweetness arose; it caught her ear, and she became once more fixed by the spell of such enchanting harmony. Alas! it was of more power than the call of duty over her wavering mind.

The music now seemed to come from the opposite side of the stream; and so much was her curiosity excited, that she took the resolution to try to cross it, and to find out the unseen minstrel. She looked round and perceived some large loose stones, which served, though not without risk, for stepping-stones. Serena was light of foot and very active; and so by marking well, where to venture, and springing from rock to rock, she managed to get over the stream. Again did she enter on a narrow path, and followed it for a few yards, when, on a sudden turn, she came in sight of the loveliest waterfall that she had ever seen.

It was situated at the extremity of a recess among the wildest rocks. These formed so complete an enclosure, that it was only in front facing the fall that a view of it could be gained. The cascade itself was not lofty, not above fifty or sixty feet in height; it was its form and accompaniments which rendered it of such surpassing loveliness. A few yards distant from the fall, there stood fronting it some rocks, which half way up had the appearance of a natural arch; and through this opening the foaming waters were seen leaping and dashing over the rocks, with the most beautiful effect. Thence they rushed on in the wildest tumult over vast masses of granite, which lay in the bed of the stream as if to impede its course. Here and there, occasioned by the hollows beneath, might be found a calm deep pool, undisturbed by the impetuosity of the flood.

Serena stopped, delighted with the beauty of the scene. 'This is the sweetest ravine in the world,' she said; 'such a beautiful waterfall, and the rocks so wild and broken; and all shut in to keep it, as it were, from the approach of common mortals. Surely this must be the very place in which my nurse tells me, that Merlin of old, the great magician, in the days of Prince Arthur, used to work his spells; where the Pixies make their favourite haunt, and where they are now most powerful, and, therefore, most to be feared. But that must be false; for nothing to be feared can ever come into such a charming scene as this. But I must not linger; and now to hasten back, for here no vesper-bell can be heard, nor even that delightful music which led me hither, for here the waterfall lets no music but its own meet the ear.'

Well might Serena thus admire the scene, for what she so gazed upon were the rocks and fall of St. Nectan's Kieve.

Serena gave the cascade one last farewell look, and then turned to retrace her steps; but, at a short distance from that spot, she found it impossible to proceed without the danger of stepping upon a human being, who lay outstretched, with a lute by his side, on the narrow path under the rocks, and so close to the water's edge, that no space was left for her to glide by without disturbing him. She paused a moment; her eyes became as much fascinated by the beautiful appearance of the sleeping figure, as her ears had before been charmed by the mysterious music.

It was a strange place for repose. The sleeper was a young man with handsome features and light brown curly hair. His attire was at once rich and elegant. He wore such a cloak and vest as Serena had never before seen; the plumage of the finest birds seemed to have been used to give it splendour. And then the cap on his head, and the tiara which was bound around his brows, was so radiant and glittering with jewels, that they looked as if diamonds, and emeralds, and rubies, and sapphires had been clustered together so as to emulate in the manner of their arrangement the colours of the butterfly's wing.

Serena gazed till her admiration of the manly beauty and splendid attire of the youthful sleeper became as great as that which she had felt, a little while before, for the music; and far exceeded her admiration of the beauties of the scene. She thought that, if ever she married, it should be to just such a beautiful youth; and then his dress was so graceful, so rich; and as for his tiara, it would be the prettiest thing imaginable to have just such another to bind around her own dark and flowing hair. She felt quite sure none but a prince could altogether be so charmingly dressed, and so handsome; and he it must be who had produced from that lute such exquisite tones.

Serena was now in no hurry to pass on, but looked about her, and seeing an opening in some rocks near at hand, that were overshadowed by thick and pendant boughs, she determined to conceal herself and to survey more at her leisure the noble features and the splendid adornments of the. sleeper; hoping that, when he awoke, he would again touch the strings of his lute. The vesper bell was forgotten; and O to think from what a cause! Serena had given herself up to the influence of a vain curiosity! Soon had she cause to rue her folly; for most sadly was she beguiled by what could be nothing more than an illusion to ensnare and deceive her.

After a while, a thick mist suddenly fell like a cloud over every object around her. The very rocks and trees which sheltered her were no longer visible: The wind moaned, and the river rushed along in tumult as the roar of the waterfall became loud as rolling thunder. Serena trembled in every limb; her heart beat quick; she did not know what to do. She dared not move from the spot of her concealment. She was on the verge of despair, when gradually the mist rose like a veil that had been thrown over the landscape, and now raised by an invisible hand. The rocks, woods, and waterfall once more were distinctly seen, but under a melancholy aspect; no sun-beam fell upon them; all was shadow and gloom. She looked down on the narrow pathway; but neither the beautiful sleeping youth, nor the lute by his side were to be seen; they were gone; and she saw only the broken and mossy rocks wet with the spray and foam of the stream!

At length she arose, retraced her steps, and approached the chapel; but the vesper bell had long ceased ringing, and the doors of the chapel were closed--closed indeed, for the vesper service had been concluded half an hour before she reached the spot. Serena felt ashamed of her folly; and she added to it by keeping the knowledge of it confined to her own bosom; for neither to Father Hilary, nor to the nurse did she tell what had happened.

She was, however, often seen stealing down the pathway. that led to St. Nectan's Kieve; for by a strange fascination she was fond of going there alone; although it was in that spot she first received those impressions which now rendered her so melancholy and unhappy. At length Father Hilary saw something was the matter, and obtained from her a confession of the truth, but only in part told; for she confined herself to the statement of having wasted her time in wandering up to the waterfall in Nectan's Kieve, and being too late for the vespers. She blushed, but was so ashamed to confess how much she had been led astray, that she said not one word about the musician, his attire, or the music. But Father Hilary was quite sufficiently shocked by what she confessed, and imposed upon her a very severe penance, namely, that she should take the ten marks given to her by the Baron to buy a splendid dress to wear at a high festival to be held at the castle, and should expend the same in the purchase of a silver bell, on which she must cause to be engraved an image of herself attired as a penitent, with her hair hanging down her back, and carrying a taper in her hand, in token of sorrow for what she had done amiss. Serena obeyed, and purchased the silver bell. This Father Hilary presented in her name to the little chapel situated on the hill above St. Nectan's Kieve.

But though this was done, and though Serena had worn her old robes at the high festival of Tintagel, to the amusement of all her gaily-clad young friends, who tittered at her shabby apparel and envied her pretty looks, and though she had taken care that her many visits to the waterfall should never again interfere with the hour of ringing the vesper bell; yet was she dull and melancholy. Her spirits flagged, indeed they had never returned with their natural vivacity since that unlucky day on which she committed so great a fault. Still she longed and sighed once more to hear the charming music, and to see the handsome and gaily dressed minstrel. But she was always disappointed in her hopes and expectations.

At length she became so unhappy that she told all her secret to nurse Judy. Now, nurse Judy, though good-natured was not a very wise counsellor, for fearing Father Hilary would put the young lady to a more severe penance than the former did he know all the truth, she gave her very wrong advice as will presently be seen.

177

She told Serena that she was convinced all that had happened to her was a Pixy delusion, brought about by some of those malignant and spiteful beings, who it was well known were powerful in St. Nectan's Kieve, and more especially over anyone who had been negligent in the performance of their duty. She did not doubt that the music was the work of their spells; and as to the beautiful musician, she felt certain that he was nothing more than some mischievous imp, who had assumed that appearance on purpose to deceive her.

In order therefore to counteract these spells, she persuaded Serena to go and consult old Swillpot, the famous Cornish wizard, who dwelt near the waterfall at St. Nectan's Kieve, and who, nurse Judy said, was noted for being a kind wizard in his way, that was if he entertained no spite against the person who came to consult him; and more especially if the individual gave him a purse full of money, and a jar of strong rich mead, which had been made at the full of the moon (then considered the best time for making it), and was three years old at least. Judy declared, that she had some spiced mead called metheglin in her own particular cupboard which had been made under all the quarters of the moon, and old Swillpot should have that.

Serena, though not without fear, took all the money she had and put it into her purse; she took also Judy's jar of metheglin, which was so large she found it difficult to carry it under her cloak, and set out for the wizard's dwelling.

A very poor and miserable cottage was not the most agreeable place for so delicate a young lady as Serena to visit; but she was unhappy and wanted relief, and so she did not care to be nice, but after a gentle rap at once entered the dwelling. She was civilly received by old Swillpot, more especially when he handled the purse, and took the jar of metheglin, and with a good-humoured chuckle tucked it under his arm. He then bade Serena sit down, and he would presently talk with her.

Old Swillpot had not much the look of a wizard, for he was stout and burly, had a round full face, not unlike the moon (as that luminary is painted on the face of a clock), a very round red nose, and a beard so thick and long it reached quite down to his waist. He was in an exceeding good humour, placed himself at the head of a little table, produced a brown loaf and some Cornish cheese, as hard as if it had been cut out of the rocks, or from one of the Cornish mines, bustled up to his cupboard, produced a couple of horn cups, opened the jar, and very heartily pressed Serena to partake with him some of her own choice metheglin. This, with a smack of the lips, he pronounced to be excellent, clear as amber, rich as the honey from which it was originally made, and fit for the king himself if he ever came into Cornwall. Serena, not to offend him, just tasted the cup, and then would have proceeded to tell her tale; butt the charms of the metheglin were so much greater than those of the young lady in the estimation of old Swillpot, that not until he had half emptied the jar would he hear a word she had to say.

At last he seemed a little boozy with the strength of the potation; as he sat, neither quite awake nor yet asleep, tapping his fingers on the table, his nose three times redder than it was before, he bade her tell her story, and gave a yawn and a lengthened hum at the end of every sentence, to let her know how very attentive he was to her discourse.

He then leaned back in his chair, looked wise, considered, made a snatch at a fine tabby cat that was rubbing herself against the side of his chair, took her up on his knee, and rubbed her hair the wrong way, as she raised up her tail till it reached his chin and brushed his beard. After consulting either his own thoughts, or the motion of the cat's tail, it was doubtful which, he very solemnly assured Serena, that all her sufferings and uneasiness proceeded from a wicked delusion - that, in fact, she had been Pixy-led in the most injurious manner. Having said this, he proceeded to the subject of her cure - to free her from the powerful spell under which she was still labouring; to cure her vain desire to hear again the mysterious music, and to see the handsome musician, which so disturbed her peace. Lastly, as what she had to do must be performed at the Kieve, and in sight of the waterfall, at the full of the moon, he offered to accompany her to the spot. As the moon would be at the full that very night, he said no time should be lost; it was therefore agreed that they should set out together. Before departing, old Swillpot tucked the jar, containing the remainder of the metheglin, under his arm, and so they speedily gained the place of their destination.

But what were the fears and astonishment of Serena, when, on arriving there, the wizard directed her to climb up to the top of the rock which forms the natural arch in front of the waterfall, and lies directly over what may truly be styled a boiling and foaming cauldron. And, when there, he directed her to perform certain magical rites to appease the Pixies; for Pixies, he still declared, had been her foes

In what all these rites consisted it is not known; but, watching the moon till a cloud passed over its face, and then repeating certain words of mysterious signification, were among them. Lastly, she was enjoined to stay on the rock till she heard, even above the fall of the water, the scream of a night-bird that was said to haunt the ravine, and which made the most dismal shrieks that could be imagined. No one knew where it had a nest. It was popularly believed to be the spirit of the great enchanter, Merlin, thus inhabiting the body of a bird for a certain term of years. Merlin, it was said, had been a cruel enemy to the Pixies. Serena was directed to watch; and when she saw something dark come sailing over the rocks above, on out-spread wings, and with loud screams prepare to dash itself into the midst of the fall, then was she to address it in a form of words, which the wizard instructed her how to repeat. This done, she might descend from the rock, and would no more be troubled with any mischievous spells or fancies.

Serena, with much fear, and a quickly-beating heart, managed to ascend the rock, and to take her perilous stand upon the natural arch above the rapid and roaring flood: she did all as commanded. At length she heard a flapping of wings, and saw the dark form of a majestic bird, whose plumage shone bright and silvery in the moonbeams, rise from among the trees. Instantly she addressed it, in a firm and plaintive tone--

'Bird of night, 'tis time to leave
Thy nest, and seek St. Nectan's Kieve;
Bird of power o'er Pixy dells,
Disenchant me from their spells.
Give me freedom from their thrall,
Ere thou seek'st yon waterfall;
Drive from me idle Fancy's mood,
Or drown my folly in the flood.'

Serena, as she spoke these last words, raised herself hastily from the summit of the rock on which she was so precariously placed. At that very moment the bird with outspread wings dashed against the moon-illumined waterfall, she lost her footing and tottered. Before she could regain her balance, old Swillpot, as fast as he could make the effort, stepped forward to give assistance. Unfortunately whilst Serena had been performing the rites he dictated, in order to keep the night air from chilling his stomach, he had emptied into it the remaining half of the jar of metheglin, so that he was a little more unsteady than before; and neither his foot in stepping, nor his hand in helping, were so much under his control as at all to be sure of their purpose; and he bungled so terribly in trying to give aid, that his foot slipped, and having caught Serena by the arm, down he pushed her; and both were soused into the water. Swillpot was nearer to the banks, and somehow or other managed to scramble out.

But not so the unfortunate young lady; she had been pushed so completely over the rock by the tipsy wizard, that she fell at once into the pool which lay immediately below it;

the most deep and dangerous in the whole course of the stream. Poor Serena was seen no more. But long did her memory survive her unhappy fate; long was her story told as a sad example of so young and so lovely a creature being led into folly by her vain and idle curiosity.

Old Swillpot, who was not of an unkind heart, though he did not possess a very clear head, was so shocked and concerned at what had happened, owing to his having bewildered his brains and rendered his footing unsteady, by making too free with the metheglin; that, as the very severest penance he could possibly inflict upon himself, he renounced strong drink for ever after. And old nurse Judy was so vexed and angry with herself for having recommended her young lady to go and consult him, and for sending such an old fool, as she called him, her best and stoutest metheglin, that she took the resolution never more to give away one drop of it to any mortal creature; and so well did she observe this determination that it never more went down any throat but her own. And as a reward for keeping so strictly her purpose, old Swillpot's red nose seemed to have passed from his face to her own.

It is said to this day, when the moon is at the full, and her beams sparkle, like filaments of diamonds on the beautiful waterfall of Nectan's Kieve, Serena's Silver Bell is heard ringing in a slow and melancholy cadence, like a funeral chime; though the chapel to which it was given has long been destroyed, and neither the belfry nor bell are any more to be found.

THE PIRATE-WRECKER AND
THE DEATH SHIP

ONE lovely evening in the autumn, a strange ship was seen at a short distance from Cape Cornwall. The little wind there was blew from the land, but she did not avail herself of it. She was evidently permitted to drift with the tide, which was flowing southward, and curving in round Whitesand Bay towards the Land's-End. The vessel, from her peculiar rig, created no small amount of alarm amongst the fishermen, since it told them that she was manned by pirates; and a large body of men and women watched her movements from behind the rocks at Caraglose. At length, when within a couple of pistol-shots off the shore, a boat was lowered and manned. Then a man, whose limited movements show him to be heavily chained, was brought to the side of the ship and evidently forced for several pistols were held at his head into the boat, which then rowed rapidly to the shore in Priest's Cove. The waves of the Atlantic Ocean fell so gently on the strand, that there was no difficulty in beaching the boat. The prisoner was made to stand up, and his ponderous chains were removed from his arms and ankles. In a frenzy of passion he attacked the sailors, but they were too many and too strong for him, and the fight terminated by his being thrown into the water, and left to scramble up on the dry sands. They pushed the boat off with a wild shout, and this man stood uttering fearful imprecations on his former comrades.

It subsequently became known that this man was so monstrously wicked that even the pirates would no longer endure him, and hence they had recourse to this means of ridding themselves of him.

It is not necessary to tell how this wretch settled himself at Tregaseal, and lived by a system of wrecking, pursued with un- heard-of cruelties and cunning. 'It 's too frightful to tell,' said local people, 'what was said about his doings. We scarcely believed half of the vile things we heard, till we saw what took place at his death. But one can't say he died, because he was taken off bodily. We shall never know the scores, perhaps hundreds, of ships that old sinner has brought on the cliffs, by fastening his lantern to the neck of his horse, with its head tied close to the forefoot. The horse, when driven along the cliff, would, by its motion, cause the lantern to be taken for the stern-light of a ship; then the vessel would come right in on the rocks, since those on board would expect to find plenty of sea-room; and, if any of the poor sailors escaped a watery grave, the old wretch would give them a worse death, by knocking them on the head with his hatchet, or cutting off their hands as they tried to grasp the ledges of the rocks.

A life of extreme wickedness was at length closed with circum- stances of unusual terror so terrible, that the story is told with feelings of awe even at the present day. The old wretch fought furiously with death, but at length the time of his departure came. It was in the time of the barley-harvest. Two men were in a field on the cliff, a little below the house, mowing. A universal calm prevailed, and there was not a breath of wind to stir the corn. Suddenly a breeze passed by them, and they heard the words, 'The time is come, but the man isn't come.'

These words appeared to float in the breeze from the sea, and consequently it attracted their attention. Looking out to sea, they saw a black, heavy, square-rigged ship, with all her sails set, coming in against wind and tide, and not a hand to be seen on board. The sky became black as night around the ship, and as she came under the cliff and she came so close that the top of the masts could scarcely be perceived the darkness resolved itself into a lurid storm-cloud, which extended high into the air. The sun shone brilliantly over the country, except on the house of the pirate at Tregaseal that was wrapped in the deep shadow of the cloud.

The men, in terror, left their work; they found all the neighbours gathered around the door of the pirate's cottage, none of them daring to enter it. The parson had been sent for by the terrified peasants, being celebrated for his power of driving away evil spirits.

The dying wrecker was in a state of agony, crying out, in tones of the most intense terror, 'The devil is tearing at me with nails like the claws of a hawk! Put out the sailors with their bloody hands!" and using, in the paroxysms of pain, the most profane language. The parson, the doctor, and two of the bravest of the fishermen, were the only persons in the room. They related that at one moment the room was as dark as the grave and that at the next it was so light that every hair on the old man's head could be seen standing on end. The parson used all his influence to dispel the evil spirit. His powers were so potent that he reduced the devil to the size of a fly, but he could not put him out of the room. All this time the room appeared as if filled with the sea, with the waves surging violently to and fro, and one could hear the breakers roaring, as if standing on the edge of the cliff in a storm. At last there was a fearful crash of thunder, and a blaze of the intense lightning. The house appeared on fire, and the ground shook, as if with an earthquake. All rushed in terror from the house, leaving the dying man to his fate.

The storm raged with fearful violence, but appeared to contract its dimensions. The black cloud, which was first seen to come in with the black ship, was moving, with a violent internal motion. over the wrecker's house. The cloud rolled together, smaller and smaller, and suddenly, with the blast of a whirlwind, it passed from Tregaseal to the ship, and she was impelled, amidst the flashes of lightning and roaring of thunder, away over the sea.

The dead body of the pirate-wrecker lay a ghastly spectacle, with eyes expanded and the mouth partly open, still retaining the aspect of his last mortal terror. As everyone hated him, they all desired to remove his corpse as rapidly as possible from the sight of man. A rude coffin was rapidly prepared and the body was carefully cased in its boards. They tell me the coffin was carried to the churchyard, but that it was too light to have contained the body, and that it was followed by a black pig, which joined the company forming the procession, nobody knew where, and disappeared nobody knew when. When they reached the church stile, a storm, similar in its character to that which heralded the wrecker's death, came on. The bearers of the coffin were obliged to leave it outside the churchyard stile and rush into the church for safety. The storm lasted long and raged with violence, and all was as dark as night. A sudden blaze of light, more vivid than before, was seen, and those who had the bravery to look out saw that the lightning had set fire to the coffin, and it was being borne away through the air, blazing and whirling wildly in the grasp of such a whirlwind as no man ever witnessed before or since.

I hope you enjoyed this small volume of Cornish Folk Tales. If you did, please spread the word to others - by word of mouth or perhaps by leaving a review on an Amazon website.

There are two more volumes planned in the series of Cornish Tales. The next will be Cornish Fairy Tales and that will be followed by Cornish Legends.

A website - www.cornishtales.com - will carry details.

Merryn Petrock

If you are looking for modern stories set in Cornwall and featuring Cornish Folklore suitable for younger readers may I suggest you search out a book called "The Hollow Sword" by Carenza Bassett and its companion volumes that make up "The Kernow Trilogy"

Made in the USA
Monee, IL
28 July 2020